NOTHING BUT NET

Also by Michael Coldwell in
the Lorimer Sports Stories series

Camp All-Star
Fast Break

NOTHING BUT NET

Michael Coldwell

James Lorimer & Company Ltd., Publishers
Toronto

James Lorimer & Company Ltd., Publishers acknowledges the support of the Ontario Arts Council. We acknowledge the financial support of the Government of Canada through the Canada Book Fund for our publishing activities. We acknowledge the support of the Canada Council for the Arts for our publishing program. We acknowledge the Government of Ontario through the Ontario Media Development Corporation's Ontario Book Initiative.

Cover Image: iStockphoto

Library and Archives Canada Cataloguing in Publication

Coldwell, Michael
    Nothing but net / Michael Coldwell.

(Sports stories)
Issued also in electronic format.
ISBN 978-1-55277-682-7

      I. Title. II. Series: Sports stories (Toronto, Ont.)

PS8555.O4326N67 2011   jC813'.54   C2010-906618-9

James Lorimer & Company Ltd.,
Publishers
317 Adelaide St. West
Suite #1002
Toronto, ON Canada
M5V 1P9
www.lorimer.ca

Distributed in the United States by:
Orca Book Publishers
P.O. Box 468
Custer, WA USA
98240-0468

Printed and bound in Canada.
Manufactured by Friesens Corporation in Altona, Manitoba, Canada in January 2011.
Job #62890

To Mom and Dad

CONTENTS

1 THE BAD NEWS BEARS

"Well?"

"Mission accomplished," giggled Chip Carson, sliding into the vinyl bus seat and high-fiving his best friend.

Trevor Huntley tried not to laugh. He still couldn't believe that Chip had pulled this stunt off. Actually, he *could* believe it. For as long as he'd known Chip there had never been a stunt that Chip couldn't pull off. "When will he find it?"

Chip studied his watch intently and held up his hand. "In about three . . . two . . . one . . . now!"

"Grooooosssss!" roared Langdon Strong. "Whoever put Jello in my sneakers is going to die!" The tall boy jumped out of his seat and started waving his gym shoes in the air. The whiteness of the basketball sneakers was marred by a trail of slimy red jelly trickling down the sides.

"Right on cue," Chip smiled.

"Epic genius," Trevor replied.

"Chip Carson, you're dead!"

"Me?" Chip turned around and looked at Langdon with his best puppy dog eyes. "What makes you think *I* did it?"

"Because," Langdon yelled back, "you do everything."

"He's got a point there," Trevor murmured.

From his seat at the front of the bus, Coach Kenny poked his young, bristly blond head up over the seat. "What's going on, guys?"

"Chip filled my sneakers with Jello," tattled Langdon.

"Objection! He has no proof of that, Your Honour," countered Chip.

"Carson, did you fill his sneakers with Jello?"

"Well, yes," admitted Chip, "but he had no right to accuse me!"

"Aw, come on, guys." Coach Kenny rolled his eyes in frustration. "Carson, clean his sneakers, would ya?"

"I consider that cruel and unusual punishment, sir, and my lawyers will be in touch."

"Clean 'em!" Coach Kenny repeated, in as stern a tone as the young man could muster.

"Yeah, clean 'em," sneered Langdon, dropping the sticky sneakers on Chip's seat.

"You must agree that your shoes did make a great Jello mold," Chip responded brightly. "After all, the mold was already in there."

Langdon stamped backed to his seat as Chip Carson set to work wiping off Langdon's sneakers with a white sweat sock.

"Well done," Trevor said finally. "A solid six point five, man." It was customary for the boys to rank their pranks out of ten.

"Only six point five?" cried Chip, tugging at his bushy, bright-red hair in disbelief. "Tough crowd." The stocky boy pretended to pout as he folded his thick legs beneath him and propped himself up in the seat.

Chip and Trevor, along with the rest of the Cape Breton High School Grizzly Bears, were headed to Halifax to play in the Nova Scotia Invitational Basketball Tournament. The event brought together teams from across the province for two days of basketball action. To say the Grizzly Bears were going into the tournament as long shots would be an understatement.

It was no secret that the Grizzly Bears were one of the worst teams in the province. In fact, they were only invited to the tournament at all because the rules said that the northeastern region must be represented, and Cape Breton High School was the only school in the northeastern region. Everyone knew how bad the Bears were — including the Bears themselves.

"So, after we lose our first game are we knocked out of the tournament, or do we have to lose another one?"

The question came from the Bears' lanky starting centre, Matt "Big" McMann. Matt was one of those guys who went through puberty at the age of four, started shaving at twelve, and now, in grade nine, could get into R-rated movies or buy dirty magazines without being asked for identification. Needless to say, this made Big one of the more popular guys on the team.

"Double elimination, Big Man," answered Chip. "Why the hurry to get home?"

Despite the fact that they were going to get slaughtered on the court, most of Chip's teammates were anxious to have fun on the road trip.

Big squinted his ice-blue eyes and nervously ran his fingers through his buzz cut. "Our biology project is due on Monday. You and I were supposed to be working on it as a team, remember?"

"That's due *this* Monday?" Chip looked as if he'd just swallowed a goldfish.

"Aw, man," Big bit his lip. "Don't tell me you forgot."

"Okay," Chip replied with a nervous laugh. "I won't tell you I forgot."

"Chip, you said you were going to take care of it. If your part isn't done, then what are we going to hand in on Monday? We're going to get an incomplete. This is terrible! I can't have an incomplete on my permanent record!" Big shook his head.

A blemish on his permanent record was, without a doubt, the worst thing that could happen to Big. Big McMann took school very seriously. In fact, the burly boy didn't get his nickname just for the size of his body — his intellect was pretty impressive too.

Chip had started calling him Big Brain after Matt McMann had aced a provincial aptitude test. The name stuck and was eventually shortened to Big. Although he was a monster on the basketball court, his real interest was physics and he had already decided that he wanted to be a mechanical engineer.

"Look, Big, don't stress it," Chip soothed. "We'll have lots of time between games, so we'll take a second to go online and Google up ourselves some brilliance."

"You better."

"Will you guys be quiet?" Chip, Big, and Trevor wheeled around to face a very sleepy-looking Langdon Strong. Langdon's squinty green eyes looked even narrower than usual and his brown hair, normally perfectly groomed, was sticking up in the back. "Yak, yak, yak. Can't you see some of us are trying to catch a nap?"

"Terribly sorry," Chip replied with mock sincerity. "Did we interrupt your beauty sleep, superstar?"

"Can that superstar crap, Carson," Langdon snapped. "You know there's only one guy on this bus that gives us half a chance of winning a game."

"Oh?" Chip looked perplexed. "Langdon, did you kidnap LeBron James again?"

"Carson, I'm the best player on this team, and if I'm going to carry you chumps on the court, I better be rested. Now zip it." Langdon flopped back into his seat and promptly closed his eyes.

It was rumoured that even his own mother couldn't stand Langdon Strong. The starting forward for the Bears was arrogant, rude, selfish, and — to top it off

— had legendary foot odour. But he was right — he was the best player on the team. Langdon was a fantastic ball-handler, had great speed, could drive to the hole, rain jumpshots from anywhere, and even dunk if he had a clear running start. Passing was the only part of Langdon's game that was questionable. Not because he wasn't good at it, but because no one had ever actually seen him pass. In recent Grizzly history, a Langdon Strong assist was about as rare as a team victory.

No one minded letting Langdon sleep. For the past four hours they had listened to his constant boasting. He had made it clear that he intended to score all of the Bears' points and win the tournament MVP award. What irritated the rest of the team was that Langdon could do it.

For the next half-hour, the yellow school bus rumbled along the highway toward Halifax. Simple bungalows and farms dotted the rural scenery outside the bus windows, while grey clouds filled the chilly-looking sky overhead. When they reached the next town, Coach Kenny announced they were going to stop for lunch.

"Yummy . . . greasy burgers," cried Chip, as the bus pulled into the parking lot of Super Burger. "I play better when my arteries are clogged with cholesterol."

"I think your brain is clogged with cholesterol some days, Carson," Coach Kenny joked as the boys piled off the bus.

"At least I have a brain, Coach," Chip joked with a smile.

Chip really liked the team's young instructor. He was more like another player on the team than a coach, always goofing around with the guys and making jokes. There was probably a lot of truth to the rumour that Coach Kenny only got his job because he was married to Amy Taylor, the daughter of the CBHS principal. Kenny was a lot of fun, but he wasn't exactly the sharpest pencil in the pack. In fact, there were penguins that knew more about basketball than he did. Then again, who on the Bears actually cared about basketball?

"Hey, where's Langdon?" Kenny asked as the boys assembled in the parking lot.

"He's asleep, Coach," Chip piped up.

"Shouldn't we wake him?"

"No. Langdon specifically requested that we don't disturb him, didn't he, Tee?"

"Indeed he did," Trevor replied.

The two exchanged an evil grin.

"Well, okay then," Coach Kenny looked unsure. "Bus leaves in twenty-five minutes."

2 BURGER BULLIES

When the guys stepped off the bus, they immediately noticed two things. First, cows and chickens outnumbered people on the outskirts of Truro, and second, a schoolyard basketball hoop stood right next to the Super Burger where they had stopped to eat.

"Hey, you guys want to play some pickup?" Trevor asked.

"Shouldn't we save our energy for the tournament?" suggested Chip sarcastically.

"Yeah, right," replied Big. "If I'm tired maybe I can ride out the humiliation on the bench."

"Hey, Coach, we're going to play a quick game of pickup, all right?"

"Whatever," Coach Kenny ran his hand through his sand-coloured hair and tried to look gruff. "That bus is leaving in twenty-five minutes and I don't care if I'm the only one on it."

A few boys straggled into the fast food joint, and Chip looked around for someone to join his friends in a game of two-on-two.

"Hey, Morrison, quick game of pickup?"

Jim Morrison was a tall, dark-haired boy with a perfect smile and easy manner. He was sitting on the curb of the parking lot slowly picking out a rock ballad on his guitar.

"Can't, man," Morrison replied, pointing at the cowboy boots on his feet. "No sneakers."

"Well, go get them," Big suggested.

"I didn't bring them," Morrison replied.

"You didn't bring your sneakers?" Big was incredulous.

"Nope."

"You do realize that we're going to a tournament, don't you?"

Morrison nodded.

"And you do know that we're going to play basketball at this tournament, right?"

"Yep."

"Okay, I'll bite," Chip said finally. "Why didn't you bring your sneakers?"

"Well, Coach never puts me in the game, so I figured what's the point?"

Chip, Trevor, and Big thought about it for a second then nodded. Jim Morrison sat on the bench so much he was more likely to get splinters in his behind than break a sweat.

"Yeah, but Morrison, what if Big and Langdon and

Trevor and me get fouled out, and a few more guys get hurt, kicked out of the game, or abducted by aliens — then you'd be right in there!"

"That's a chance I'm willing to take," Morrison strummed a chord on his guitar. "Hey. I'm writing a love song for Stephanie Sherman. You guys want to hear it?"

"No," the boys chorused in unison. With his good looks and his skill with a guitar, Jim Morrison was always going out with a new girl. Nobody could figure out why Morrison wasted every Friday night taking a girl out when the rest of the guys were hanging out at the mall, having spitball fights at Barry's Burger Palace, or doing other fun stuff.

"Enough talking," Chip declared. "Let's play. Me and Morrison take."

Morrison protested a little, but Chip was already dragging him onto the court.

"Okay, who gets first ball?" Trevor asked, peeling off his bulky grey sweatshirt and brushing a stray fuzz ball from his short afro.

"Big, what's the category?"

"Canadian geography." The tall boy declared. First ball was always decided by a correct answer to one of Big's trivia questions. "Which is the largest of the Great Lakes?"

"Lake Ontario!" Chip cried.

"Wrong," Trevor gloated, snatching the ball. "It's Lake Superior."

"I protest," Chip replied. "You said Canadian geography. Aren't some of those lakes in the U.S.?"

"Whatever," Big waved off Chip's protest. "Next time the category will be intellectually-challenged sore losers and the answer will be Chip Carson. Now let's play."

"All right," conceded Chip, checking the ball with Trevor at the top of the key.

Trevor wasted no time making his move. With a little stutter-step that left Chip rooted to the ground, Trevor scooted by to score the uncontested layup.

Slapping five with Big, Trevor took the ball at the top once again. "Hey, Big," he called, scrunching up his nose and sniffing like a bloodhound. "You smell something?"

"Like what?"

"Sort of smells like burnt toast."

"Ha ha," Chip laughed sarcastically. "Enjoy that one hoop, Tee, 'cause it's the only one you're getting."

Trevor tried to put another move on his compact friend, but Chip quickly shuffled his feet and cut off Trevor's lane to the basket. Trevor zipped a pass over to Big who was powering his way into the low post. Poor Morrison looked like a man caught in a strong wind as Big bulldozed his way to the basket for an easy score.

"What are we playing to?" Morrison asked, discouraged.

"Seven? Then we'll go eat."

"Tough defence, Morrison," Chip cheered. "Let's go."

Right off the check, Trevor jab-stepped to the left and drove right. Chip didn't bite on the fake and made the clean steal as Trevor ran by.

Dribbling the ball by the foul line, Chip looked to make a pass to Morrison, but the dark-haired boy was busy wrestling with Big under the hoop — and losing badly. Ignoring his teammate, Chip dribbled the ball between his legs twice, took a quick step back behind the three-point arc, and drained the jumpshot.

"Nothing but net!" Chip cried, raising his arms like a referee signalling three points.

"Luck," smiled Trevor.

"Shut up! I've been practising those."

"Whatever," Trevor rolled his eyes.

Still with the ball, Chip fired a pass to Morrison, who had popped out on the wing. Not waiting to see what Morrison was going to do, Chip made a sharp cut to the hoop, waving his arm and calling for the ball. Morrison dumped a pass to the cutting Chip, who went up for a layup, only to have Trevor slap the ball away into the next time zone.

"Rejection!" taunted Trevor, waving his hands in Chip's face.

Chip kicked the dirt. "I hate being short."

"Just keep firing those jumpers and you'll be okay," Trevor said, extending his hand to Chip. As Chip went to slap five, Trevor pulled his hand back. "Psych!"

The boys started laughing and Chip play-punched his friend.

"Hey, chumps, keep practising! Not like it'll do you any good!"

The Bears spun around to see who was yelling at them. In the Super Burger parking lot, beside their beat-up yellow school bus, was a sleek charter bus with members of the Cartier Academy team disembarking. Cartier Academy was the top-notch private school in Nova Scotia. They had won the provincial tournament two years in a row and they always had a strong team. They were also a bunch of jerks.

Chip and his friends stopped and stared as the other team laughed and made rude gestures in their direction.

"There's a class act," Big observed.

"Ignore them," said Morrison.

"Yeah, let's go grab something to eat," growled Chip.

Inside the Super Burger, the boys were hit with the sound of beeping cash registers and the delicious smell of greasy burgers.

"Hmmm, let's see," Chip said, approaching the counter and eyeing the menu board on the wall. "Hamburger, cheeseburger, double cheeseburger, megaburger, chicken burger, fish burger, junior burger platter, jumbo burger platter, fries, onion rings, chicken nuggets, garden salad, Caesar salad, hot apple pie, ice cream sundae, milkshake, and a Coke."

"Your order comes to $82.14," droned the polyester-clad burger jockey behind the counter.

Chip gave the guy a strange look. "Oh, I'm sorry," he replied, trying to keep a straight face. "I was just reading the menu. I'll have a cheeseburger and Coke." Chip turned and slapped five with Trevor as the cashier rolled his eyes.

Bringing trays of hot greasy food to a table at the back of the burger joint, Chip, Trevor, Big, and Morrison were the last of the Bears in Super Burger. Looking around the bustling restaurant, Trevor noticed that all of their teammates were already on the bus.

"What's the time, Big?"

"Relax, we still have five minutes."

"You don't think Coach would really leave without us, do you?" asked Morrison, a little worried.

"Don't be dumb," Chip said, choking down his burger. "I don't think Coach would leave without three of his starting lineup."

"Maybe he doesn't know we're on his starting line-up?" Trevor suggested.

Chip mulled this over. "Definite possibility," he said finally, shoving half a burger into his mouth. "Better eat up, guys," he garbled.

"Done," sang out Morrison, crumpling his Super Burger wrapper and sliding out of the plastic booth. "I got to go to the bathroom."

"Thanks for the info," Trevor replied, slurping the

remains of his soft drink.

The rest of the boys were just collecting their garbage and about to leave when three guys wearing shiny black and purple Cartier Academy Wildcat team jackets strutted over to their table.

"You guys from the Cape Breton Grizzly Bears?" asked the small, wiry boy in the lead. It was clear from the tone of his voice that he didn't want to make polite conversation.

Chip stared daggers at the Wildcats before flashing a big grin. "Why yes, we are. I suppose you gentlemen are looking for autographs." Chip turned to his teammates. "Everywhere we go, guys, we have fans. It's nice to be loved, huh?"

Trevor smiled at Chip. It was easy for the boys to be cocky with a six-foot-two bulldozer like Big at the table.

"You guys stink," sneered the wiry boy, causing his two friends to start laughing.

"Wow, you're a real comedian. You should take your act on the road some day," Chip replied, pointing to the door. "Like maybe now?"

"And if we don't?" challenged the wiry Wildcat.

Big tensed and shot a glance at Chip who shook his head. Chip could be a smart aleck, but he wasn't about to start a fist fight in the middle of Super Burger.

"Look, guys, I think we're getting off to a bad start here," Chip smiled broadly. "I'm Chip and you are . . ." Chip looked at the name patch on the short guy's jacket, "Cha. Nice to meet you, Cha."

"Chad," growled the Wildcat. "My name's Chad. The *d* fell off my jacket."

"Whatever, Cha," Chip continued. "And these here are my teammates, Trevor and Big."

"Big?" scoffed Chad, staring down at the Grizzly Bear centre. Sitting at the table, Big actually looked average-sized. "What type of a name is Big? Is that like Big Loser? Or maybe Big Moron?"

"How about Big Jerk," chimed in one of Chad's teammates.

Chip just shook his head as Big slowly unfolded himself until he was standing at full height.

"I think it's like Big Mistake," said Chip calmly, as Big stared down at the surprised Wildcats. "As in you made a big mistake making him mad."

Big scowled at Chad and his friends. Although Big was so harmless that he had to be excused when his class was dissecting frogs in biology, his thick eyebrows, close-cropped hair and larger-than-normal size made him look like a Frankenstein monster glaring down at the Wildcats.

"Well, we'd love to stay and chat, boys," said Chip, looking at his watch. "But I think it's time for you guys to leave, right?"

"You guys suck," Chad growled, as the Wildcats beat a hasty retreat.

Big grinned and slapped five with the rest of the guys.

"I think we should go," Trevor suggested.

"I think you're right," Big agreed.

Chip looked disgusted. "I think they're right. We do suck."

★ ★ ★

"So what's wrong with you?" said Trevor, breaking twenty minutes of silence as the yellow school bus bounced down a two-lane highway an hour outside of Halifax.

"Sorry," replied Chip. "I'm just quiet."

"You're more than quiet," Trevor laughed. "Quiet for you is taking a breath between sentences. What's wrong?"

Chip smiled. Trevor knew him too well. "I'm just thinking about those clowns back there at Super Burger."

"Don't worry about them. They're a bunch of losers, bro."

"I know that, Tee, but so are we." Chip shook his head. "I mean, nobody ever gives us any respect and it just makes me mad sometimes."

"Yeah, but what can you do?" Trevor sighed. "I mean, I have a lot of fun being on this team, but none of it comes from being on the court."

Chip nodded thoughtfully and stared out the bus window. Trevor was absolutely right, and while Chip made more jokes than anyone about how bad the Grizzly Bears were, deep down he wished they were good. He would love to play for a basketball powerhouse, wearing shiny uniforms and riding to tournaments in big chartered buses. He would give anything to walk into a dressing room after a game cheering, rather than making jokes to cover the embarrassment of losing by forty points.

The silence was broken by a loud yawn coming from the seat behind them.

"Well, I must thank you morons for being so quiet. I had a great nap." Langdon Strong poked his head over the seat and stretched his arms. "But now I'm starved. When are we stopping to eat?"

Chip and Trevor looked at each other and slapped five.

"Well done," Chip said.

"At least a seven," replied Trevor.

3 AN UN-BEAR-ABLE DEFEAT

"Coach, you didn't mean to do it," Chip soothed, as the bus raced along Highway 102.

"Yeah, but I still left him there." Coach Kenny shook his head glumly.

"But we went back and got him as soon as you realized," Trevor replied. "Morrison was there for less than an hour."

"I didn't mean to forget him," Coach Kenny mumbled.

"We know, Coach." Chip patted him on the back. As Chip and Trevor sat down, they caught Langdon Strong glaring at them.

"You guys are a couple of sweeties," he growled. Langdon was even more of a jerk when he was hungry.

"Too bad we couldn't have left you at Super Burger instead," Chip sang cheerily. "That would be my definition of a happy meal."

Langdon just glared, and within the hour the aging yellow school bus was rumbling along the streets of Halifax.

Queen Elizabeth High School was located right downtown. The run-down brick building stood across the street from an old hotel where the boys would be bunked. In the school's parking lot, team buses and minivans were corralled at the far end, with spectators' cars jammed throughout the lot. Even though this was just a school tournament, it was very popular with the locals. The Cape Breton Bears were going to play in front of real live fans.

"All right, gentlemen," Coach Kenny called out. "We're here. Now grab your gear and follow me. We're running late and we've got to check in with the tournament organizers and get changed. Our game starts in less than an hour. After the game, we'll move our stuff to the hotel. Any questions?"

"Yeah," piped up Big. "Who do we play in the first game?"

"Not that it matters," mumbled Trevor.

"A school from Windsor," replied Coach Kenny. "They'll be tough."

"Big surprise there," groaned Morrison.

The rest of the Grizzly Bears grumbled their discontent.

"Hey, guys," shouted the coach. "Don't worry about it. Let's just get out there and do our best, have some fun, blah, blah, blah. You guys know the speech. Now let's move it."

"Yeah, I could have some fun," commented Trevor

as the boys trudged across the parking lot toward certain basketball humiliation. "I could go to the mall, hit the arcade, maybe take in a movie. That would be fun, but it wouldn't leave much time for playing hoops."

Chip didn't answer. The hood of his sweatshirt was pulled up against the wind and he was busy grooving to tunes being injected into his skull via a pair of headphones. Chip had been to a basketball tournament before.

The front entrance of the school was packed with people. Everywhere you looked there were basketball players listening to headphones and wearing enormous sweatshirts.

Coach Kenny approached the organizers' table and announced that the Cape Breton Bears had arrived.

"So you guys are the big, bad Grizzly Bears?" The fat, sweaty man behind the check-in table smiled a toothy grin. "I heard you guys got a good team this year. A real wild bunch of athletes." The fat man rolled back in his chair and let out a wheezing sound that passed for a laugh.

"Yeah," Coach Kenny shrugged and tried to share in the fat man's laugh, even though it was clearly at the expense of his team. "So, which locker room do we have?"

"'Fraid both locker rooms are in use," replied the red-faced organizer.

"Fine, what classroom can we change in?"

"'Fraid they're all being used too."

"So where do you expect my boys to get ready for our game?" Coach Kenny inquired, a little confused.

The fat man shrugged his wide shoulders and stared long and hard at his wrist watch. "Well, according to me, you boys should have been here about an hour ago."

"Yeah, sorry about that. We kind of had to make an unscheduled stop," Coach Kenny replied sheepishly. "So is there anywhere we can change?"

The man grinned at another tournament official who was leaning against the wall sipping a cup of coffee. "Dunno. Maybe you could change on your bus."

"Aw, c'mon," replied Coach Kenny lowering his voice so his team wouldn't hear. "I can't have my boys change on the bus. The bus is parked half a kilometre away and it's freezing out. Help me out here, would you?"

"Sorry," droned the man behind the table, his eyes glazing over, clearly showing that he couldn't care less.

Coach Kenny opened his mouth to voice another plea, but he knew when he was defeated. The young coach slumped his shoulders and turned to face his team. "Um, fellas, I'm afraid they don't have any locker rooms for us to get changed in."

"Where we gonna get dressed, Coach?" Morrison called.

Coach Kenny bit his lip. "I guess we'll have to get changed on the bus," he said finally.

"The bus?" Morrison couldn't believe his ears.

"It's cold outside, dude," came an obvious observation from the back.

"We'd have to walk back in our shorts," Big protested.

"Where do we go at halftime?"

"Sorry, fellas," Coach Kenny threw up his hands. "I'm open to suggestions."

Chip gestured at the bustling front foyer of the school. "Why don't we get dressed right here?" he said loudly.

"Can it, Carson," Coach Kenny sighed. "Any serious ideas?"

"I am serious," Chip continued. "Look, there's lots of room here."

"And it's warm." A murmur of agreement went up from the team. Chip and Trevor immediately began pulling off their sweatshirts.

"You guys can't get changed in the front entrance," the tournament organizer said sternly. "It's not decent."

"Sure we can," called Chip, starting to pull off his nylon track pants. "Right, fellas?"

There was a chorus of agreement and giggles as some of the guys started undressing in the hall.

"Beats the cold," commented Morrison, already bare-chested.

"Hope I remembered to wear underwear," laughed Trevor, sitting in the middle of the floor and prying off his sneakers.

"Let's get naked!" yelled Chip.

"Wait!" yelled the fat man, catching a worried look from a mother passing through the mob of disrobing boys. "Coach, please control your kids."

"He can't control this bunch of wild athletes," said Morrison, shrugging helplessly.

Coach Kenny took a step toward the man and started talking in a real low voice. "You know, in five minutes you'll have fifteen naked kids in the registration area of your tournament." Kenny paused to let the image settle into the mind of the tournament staffer. "You sure you don't want to have another look for a change room?"

The red-faced man nodded silently and rushed over to talk to the other organizer, who had now finished his coffee. After a few seconds he came back.

"You guys can get changed in Room 217. It's just down the hall from the gym, on the left."

"Oh, look at that, fellas," Coach Kenny smiled broadly. "They found a room for us."

The Bears laughed loudly as they lugged their gym bags down the hallway and into Room 217.

"Let's hear it for Coach!" shouted Trevor when the whole team was in the room. The wild yelling was cut short by Coach Kenny.

"Cool it, fellas. Carson, if you ever pull a stunt like that again I will personally kick your butt all the way back home," Coach Kenny glared around the room. "Imagine, making fools of yourselves out there in front of everyone. Just terrible." He shook his head. "Now get your game gear on. I'll be back in a minute."

As the Coach stormed out of the room, some of the players could have sworn they saw a hint of a smile on his face. The door had barely swung shut when Langdon Strong strutted to the front of the room.

"All right, guys, listen up," Langdon had taken off his headphones and was about to deliver his regular pre-game anti-pep talk. "We don't have a chance out there if I don't have a good game. And I can only have a good game if you guys pass me the ball."

Chip couldn't stand it. "Hey, Langdon, will you be wearing a regular uniform this game, or will you be wearing your red tights and cape?"

A few guys snickered, but not everyone. Langdon was hard to take, but everyone knew he could back up his boasting on the court. The Bears would run their offence through him and hope that he played well enough for them to pull off an upset.

"Derrick, Trevor, you guys have to give me the ball when I'm in the deep corner. I can hit that shot all day, so make sure you're awake," Langdon continued, strutting back and forth at the front of the room. "If we're on a fast break, make sure I have the ball. I want to dunk it, so keep out of my way."

After Langdon finished his tirade, he sat down in the far corner, turned the volume on his headphones to high, and closed his eyes. He was getting psyched. The rest of the guys were doing everything they could to take their mind off of the upcoming game.

"Hey, Taps, what's the scoop on these guys?" Big asked, tugging on a bright white tube sock.

Taps was the last guy to make the Grizzly Bears. He got his nickname because, as the twelfth man, he served as more of a manager and water boy than actual player. The fact that he couldn't do a layup to save his life didn't take away from the fact that he was easily the most enthusiastic guy on the team. And he knew more about basketball than anyone else. He could tell you where any NBA player had gone to high school. He knew what every college player's major was. He also knew everything about the teams that the Bears were going to play.

The rest of the guys didn't really care about the endless stream of statistics that Taps constantly spouted, but they liked the guy, so they tolerated it.

"Well," said Taps happily, snapping his prescription sports goggles tightly around his head. "The Windsor Warlords are a tough team. Number two in the league, in fact."

"Best player?"

"Mouse Mannick, number twelve, guard."

"Mouse?"

"Yep," replied Taps. "His teammates call him Mouse because he always wears socks with Mickey Mouse on them. Don't be fooled though, he's a player. We also have to look out for their power forward, Jack Lazarenko. He's a tough farm boy. He doesn't have great height, but he's got more muscles than a seafood buffet. They've got lots of good guys coming off the bench, too."

"So what you're basically saying, Taps," Chip observed, fidgeting with the controls of his iPod, "is that the whole team is good."

"Basically," Taps nodded sadly.

"Aw man," Morrison groaned. "We are going to get creamed."

"All right, guys," Coach Kenny shouted, bursting back into the classroom. "Warm-ups have started. Get your butts out on the court."

A few of the Grizzly Bears finished tucking in their forest-green uniform tops. As the team straggled down the hallway toward the gym, Chip thought they looked like sheep headed for the slaughterhouse.

The Bears' entrance into the Queen Elizabeth High School gymnasium was met with a smattering of applause from the sparse crowd that was on hand. This was an unimportant game to them. The Bears were ranked last and everyone knew that the Windsor team was going to trample them.

"All right, guys. Let's try not to embarrass ourselves," shouted Langdon.

"Hey, we showed up didn't we?" grumbled Morrison, untucking his uniform top, which was too small for him. "The damage is done."

The boys were still warming up when suddenly loud techno music starting pounding over the gymnasium's sound system. The crowd started cheering and the Windsor Warlords burst into the gym. The twelve players raced onto the court, running in step. They ran two laps around the gym, circling the Bears, before jogging to their own end of the floor where they started their intricate warm-up routine.

Wearing matching tracksuits and serious game faces, the Windsor team looked as if they were about to play in the NBA finals. If the Bears were intimidated before the game, they were devastated after seeing the competition.

"Look at those guys," said Trevor, shaking his head in awe as the Warlords zipped around the court with machine-like precision. "Are they human or, like, basketball cyborgs?"

"Don't look at them," ordered Langdon. "Don't let them think we're intimidated."

"But Langdon," chimed in Morrison, "we *are* intimidated."

When the buzzer finally sounded to end the warm-up, the Bears straggled off the court with so little enthusiasm, they looked like they were about write a math exam, not play a basketball game.

"Langdon, Big, Trevor, Chip, Derrick, you're out there. I want to see some hustle and some smart plays." Coach Kenny crowded his five starters together and flashed them a sympathetic smile. "Guys, just do your best and try to have some fun out there, all right?"

As both teams crowded around the jump ball circle for the opening tip, Chip noticed that Taps was right. The muscle-bound Jack Lazarenko had more ripples than a lake on a windy day. He also looked as if his IQ test had come back negative.

Mouse was also on the court. He was a squinty-eyed kid, with tousled brown hair and rail-thin legs. His socks did indeed have a big, smiling Mickey Mouse on them. Chip wondered if they were washed before every game.

The referee tossed up the jump ball. Big out-stretched the Windsor centre and tipped the ball back to Langdon.

The Bears' star streaked down the sideline and soared in for a layup before the Windsor players had even gotten back on defence.

The Bears' bench cheered half-heartedly as the scoreboard lit up. They had a two to nothing lead, but it was all Windsor after that.

The Bears were helpless as Windsor ran their set half-court offence every time they came down the floor. It was a simple set play in which the Warlords passed the ball around, with every player getting involved. With so many passes and picks, there were plenty of good shots to be taken.

"C'mon guys," pleaded Coach Kenny from the

sideline. "They're doing the same darn play every time they come down the floor! Let's help out on defence."

For the Bears, helping out on defence meant yelling at the guy who had made a mistake on the play.

"Would you guard him!?" shouted Langdon, as Jack Lazarenko dropped in another layup.

Big pointed to the Windsor player who had screened him. "I got picked off," protested the large boy, as he prepared to throw the ball back inbounds. "You could help out, you know!"

"You're big, fight through the picks," yelled a frustrated Trevor.

"Shut up, Tee. As if your defence is really stellar," retorted Big. "You look like you're moving in slow motion."

"Hey, fellas, I hate to interrupt," said a grey-shirted referee. "But are you going to play or sit here and fight with each other?"

"Yeah," called Chip. "Hurry up and give the ball to Langdon, so we can stand around and watch him take another shot."

It was true. While four of the Windsor players were serious scoring threats, the Bears were using only one option. Big would inbound the ball to Langdon. Langdon would run downcourt and either pull up for a three-point jumpshot, or drive through three defenders for a wild layup attempt. No matter how good Langdon was, the Bears couldn't win playing one-on-five.

Even if Langdon was constantly heaving up errant shots, his teammates kept feeding him the ball. Trevor could nail a jumpshot from anywhere in practice, but he was trigger-shy in a game. Big could collect rebounds the way some people collect stamps, but he wasn't a scorer. Chip was easily the quickest guy on the team and he was good at getting the offence going, but with everyone standing around watching Langdon, he really didn't have anything to do.

As a result, the Bears were in self-destruct mode. They were also down by twenty-three points at halftime.

Coach Kenny didn't know what to say. "Look, guys, we're getting killed out there. Anybody have any ideas as to what we can do to get back in this game?"

"I'm trying, Coach," Langdon whined. "But I can't score if no one passes to me."

"Whatever!" cried Chip. "You're a total ball-hog."

Langdon opened his mouth to say something, but the coach interrupted.

"Can it, guys." Coach Kenny held up his hands. "Carson, let's keep Langdon involved in the offence. Langdon, I want to see good shots out there."

Chip rolled his eyes.

"All right, guys." Coach Kenny spoke in a low voice to his starting five. "Let's play a smart second half and maybe we won't get our butts kicked here. If you guys don't lose by more than ten, I'll buy everyone pizza tonight."

Big perked up, mildly interested. "With how many toppings?"

The buzzer rang before Coach Kenny could reply. "And Carson," he shouted as the boys trotted back out on the floor. "You've got three fouls. Let's not pick up any more cheap ones."

The second half started with all of the drama of the first. Mouse raced the ball down the court and set the offence. The Windsor team would make a few crisp passes, find a gap in the Bears' defence, and score the easy hoop. It was a maddeningly predictable occurrence.

Chip was particularly annoyed because he was guarding Mouse. As the quickest guy on the Bears, Chip hated being too slow to cover the slick Windsor guard.

"Set it up," cried Mouse, waving his arm in a circular motion as the Warlords came down the floor, once again on the attack.

Chip crouched low and set his feet in a perfect defensive position. Mouse glared at Chip and motioned for his teammates to clear out from the left side of the floor. Mouse wanted to take Chip one-on-one.

"Screen left," yelled Trevor, as a freight train wearing a Windsor uniform set a pick on Chip's left side.

Sliding off the screen, Chip picked up Mouse as he was making his move to the hoop. Mouse had turned his back toward the basket and was bulling his way toward it. Chip set his hand on Mouse's hip to check the boy in place.

The referee let loose with a shrill blast on his whistle.

"Hands off him, number twenty-one," called the referee as he trotted over to the scorers' table. "That's a foul on number twenty-one green," he called.

Chip couldn't believe it and neither could Coach Kenny.

"I barely touched him!" protested Chip.

"Don't talk to the ref, Carson," yelled Coach Kenny. "Hey ref, he barely touched him!"

"No hand-checking," the referee said sternly.

"They've been hand-checking us all game," Chip yelled.

"Carson, shut up," growled Coach Kenny. "Ref, they've been hand-checking us all game."

The referee glared at Coach Kenny with cold, grey eyes. "That's enough out of you, Coach." A game official won't tolerate any argument and this zebra was clearly no-nonsense.

"You can't call baby fouls like that, ref," Chip shouted, treading on thin ice. "Did you forget to wear your glasses today, or what?"

Tweet! That was that. Not about to put up with Chip's lip, the referee slapped him with a technical foul and sent him to the bench.

"Aw, Carson," cried Coach Kenny, "why did you have to go and mouth off?"

"It's in my genes," snapped Chip.

Coach Kenny just shook his head. "Get on the

bench. Morrison, get in there for Chip."

Morrison was the last guy who had expected to see any action in this game. "Me, Coach?" His head popped up at the end of the bench.

"Yes! Get in there."

"Um, I can't, Coach," Morrison replied awkwardly, pointing to his feet. "I don't have my sneakers." Sure enough, even with his shorts and uniform jersey, Morrison was still wearing his beat up cowboy boots on his feet.

Coach Kenny, noticing the boots, let out a large sigh and stared up at the ceiling. He looked as if he would definitely rather be somewhere else at that moment.

4 CAFETERIA CASANOVA

As a rule, the Grizzly Bears hardly ever spent much time in their locker room. After a loss, the boys were eager to get back into their street clothes and forget about the embarrassment on the court.

Chip Carson was no exception. If his shoelace hadn't had a particularly stubborn knot in it, he would have been long gone immediately after the Bears' spectacular slaughter at the hands of the Windsor team.

Instead, Chip was the last man in the classroom. He was just packing up his gym bag and leaving when he overheard Coach Kenny talking on the pay phone just outside the door.

"Yeah, we lost . . . again," he said glumly. "Yeah, I know we got some good guys on the team . . . I don't know what the problem is. Maybe your dad is right, I'm just a lousy coach."

Chip paused and pushed the door open a crack.

"Well, I know it'll happen once we get back . . . Your dad hates me anyway. He's just looking for any excuse to give me the yank ... Get this — I'm twenty-seven years old and he says I'm not responsible enough to coach the guys ... Well, I didn't *mean* to leave the kid at Super Burger, Amy, but thanks for bringing that up. Please don't tell him about the guys undressing in the hallway ... No. No one was naked ... Oh yeah, I'm sure he'd love that ... I'm history for sure."

Chip turned and pressed his ear close to the door. He couldn't believe what he was hearing. Sure, the Bears were a pretty bad team, but how could Coach Kenny manage a bunch of guys who didn't want to be coached?

"Yeah," Kenny said finally. "I guess you're right. I won't worry about it. Maybe when we get back I'll just quit and save your old man the trouble of finding some excuse to fire me."

Coach Kenny not coaching the Bears! Chip shuddered at the thought. No more practices with long water breaks and easy scrimmages. No more sneaking away during games to tie Langdon Strong's underwear in tight knots. Chip had a flash of fear — what if the next coach actually knew something about basketball? Practices would be an endless stream of wind sprints, skills drills, dissecting the subtleties of a one-three-one full court press ... Chip stopped his nightmare. Coach Kenny must stay!

Announcing his presence with enough coughing to land most kids a day off of school, Chip burst through the door just as Coach Kenny was hanging up the phone.

The two stared at each other for a moment, Coach Kenny obviously wondering if Chip had overheard anything.

"What are you still doing here?" Coach Kenny demanded.

"I was, um, meditating," Chip scrambled.

"Meditating?"

"Yeah," Chip gained momentum. "You know, replaying the game in my mind's eye, focusing on what I can do better, and setting goals for the next time I step on the court."

Coach Kenny furrowed his brow. "When did you start doing this?"

"Right after you told us to do it."

"I never said to meditate after every game."

"Sure you did, Coach," Chip nodded his head confidently. "You give us all kinds of good ideas. Sometimes you don't even have to say it for us to know what you mean. That's how good a coach you are."

Coach Kenny looked puzzled.

"Anyway, I have to go and do my tai chi."

"Another thing I recommended?" Coach Kenny asked sarcastically.

"That's right, Coach," smiled Chip. "At least you remember that."

With that, Chip turned and hurried off down the hall. His smile faded fast. He was working on a plan.

★ ★ ★

"I think I'm in love," moaned Jim Morrison, as he stared across the QEH cafeteria with a glazed look in his eyes.

Trevor looked at his watch. "Whew, that took a whole three hours, I was beginning to think you had lost your touch."

"I don't know who she is, but I have to meet her," Morrison cooed, shaking his head to clear it.

"I'm not sure it's healthy to become so rapidly captivated by females you've never talked to, Morrison," Big offered from the far end of the table.

"Well, I guess there's only one thing to do," Morrison replied grandly. "Go talk to her."

With that, the tall boy got up and strutted toward a group of girls sitting on the other side of the cafeteria.

The Bears sat in hushed silence as Morrison neared the table. From where they were sitting, the guys could see a blond-haired girl lift her head and give Morrison a big smile.

"Never fails," Chip groaned. "I just don't get it."

"That was too easy," Trevor said.

"Wait," cried Big, seeing the smile fade from the girl's face.

Much to everyone's surprise, Morrison walked right past the smiling blond girl and took a seat at the next table.

On that side of the table was a small girl with

spiky, jet-black hair. With baggy grey pants and a tight polyester bowling shirt, her clothes looked like a cross between retro-seventies-cool and bag lady. Even from far across the room, the guys could clearly see the stud protruding from the girl's nose and the ring through her eyebrow.

"What is he doing?" Chip wondered aloud. "Big, sit down, would you? I can't see."

"I am sitting down," Big retorted. "Be quiet, would you?"

"I've got to see this." Chip hopped out of his chair and wandered over to where Morrison and his mystery lady were sitting. Being about as inconspicuous as a elephant in a ceramic shop, Chip hung around the table, taking an extremely long drink at a nearby water fountain, and listening to Morrison's performance.

"Hey there," Morrison said, extending his hand. "I'm Jim Morrison."

The girl flashed Morrison a look that was halfway between disinterest and complete nausea. "Congratulations," she said finally.

"And you are?"

"Caitlin," she replied through clenched teeth. "Can I help you?"

"Oh, I was just wondering if I was in heaven, because you look like an absolute angel." Jim flashed his perfect smile.

"Oh, that's sweet," Caitlin replied through a thin

smile. "That's so sweet I think I'm getting a cavity. Please excuse me, I'm going to my dentist now to beg him to drill out all my teeth and put me out of the complete agony caused by you sitting here."

Morrison was slightly taken aback. "Rough day, huh?"

"Yeah, I am having a rather rough day, Jim," Caitlin spat back. "It all started the day you were born and fate sent you on a cosmic collision course which has ended with you trying to talk to me. Please. Stop."

Jim Morrison was oblivious. "So, do you play for the QEH girls' basketball team?"

"Do I *look* like I play for the girls' basketball team?" Caitlin replied, tugging on the ring through her eyebrow and running her fingers through her black hair, which was streaked with purple. "I am here as punishment because, apparently, I need to be more involved with extra-curricular activities. You see, Jim, *yesterday* was a rough day. It started when I missed my bus and had to be driven to school by my freaky stepdad — twenty-five minutes of the What-Are-Going-To-Do-With-Your-Life speech. Oh God. Can I puke now, stepdaddy dearest? First period was a nightmare, too. Matthew Wamboldt started calling me the Human Pin Cushion — isn't that clever, Jim? — and much to the delight of his no-brain friends, the nickname stuck." Caitlin fingered her nose stud in frustration, but continued her angry rambling.

"I was just going to kick back at lunch, when Courtney Canfield and her band of Abercrombie-model-wannabe friends decided that I was sitting at 'their' table — mature, *n'est pas*? That was an ugly exchange, but tossing chocolate pudding all over Courtney's precious pink sweater was totally worth two weeks of detention." Caitlin fought off a smile by furrowing her brow.

"So, you see, Jim, I'm not in the best of moods because I really don't want to be here, surrounded by a bunch of bubble-brain cheerleaders and loser jocks — present company not excluded — but I have to be. I'm a tournament 'volunteer' — they gave me a cute little badge and everything. Only I'm not a volunteer, I'm a prisoner of the secondary school system, which I hate and despise, and I'm not going to take it anymore!!"

Caitlin stood up rapidly and stuffed her banana peel and muffin wrapper into her lunch bag. No doubt, she'd compost them later.

Morrison was speechless and spellbound. He couldn't take his eyes from Caitlin's lips, which were painted jet-black. She was not like any other girl he had ever met. Truth be told, Caitlin Burrack was like no other girl on the planet.

"Now, if you'll excuse me, Jim, it was a total pleasure."

★ ★ ★

"That's the girl of his fantasy?" Trevor exclaimed, voicing everyone's disbelief. "That's definitely one weird fantasy."

Chip announced his return to the table with a prolonged belch. "I think my fantasy right about now would be to play a game without Langdon Strong hogging the ball," he said, noticing the Bears' ball-hog barrelling toward their table. "It would be great to get a shot on the court."

A murmur of agreement went up from the guys just as Langdon joined them. "Sixty-two to thirty," he sneered as he sat down heavily at the head of the table. "You guys suck."

"Sorry, Langdon," snapped Chip. "Hope we didn't ruin your chance of winning the MVP award."

"I doubt that," Langdon replied snidely. "I was the best player on the court as far as I'm concerned. Besides, when I win the three-point shooting contest, I'm sure I'll turn some more heads."

"What if you don't win?"

"Who's going to beat me?" Langdon laughed. "You?"

"And if I do?" Chip replied.

"Name it," Langdon said, extending his arms and offering Chip the world.

"You mysteriously injure your ankle and sit out our next game." Chip's answer came so quickly that it was obvious it was not the first time the thought had occurred to him.

"And what happens if — when — I win?"

Chip extended his arms.

"You stop," Langdon said simply.

"Stop what?" Chip was puzzled.

Trevor broke into a grin. "Breathing, probably."

"No," Langdon continued. "You stop your wise-cracks and jokes about me. You stop making fun of me and you stop making me look like a jerk."

"But you *are* a jerk," Chip retorted, then clapped his hand over his mouth. "Sorry, comes naturally."

"Case in point," Langdon cried.

"So that stuff gets to you, huh?" Chip asked, trying not to smile.

"Of course it doesn't," Langdon sneered.

"Yeah it does."

"Does not. Shut up."

"I think it does."

"It does not!" Langdon yelled.

"Deal," Chip said finally, as Langdon continued to stare daggers at a grinning Chip.

"Chip," Big called from the end of the table.

"Yes, Big?" Chip called back, still with a smile on his face.

"When are we going to finish our biology project?"

Chip's smile faded fast. "Well, Big, I was meaning to talk to you about that . . ."

Big cocked his head and prepared himself for another classic Chip Carson excuse.

"I'm afraid they've got the Wi-Fi on lockdown in the entire school and the hotel wants seventeen bucks for Internet access, but I did hang my laptop out the window and found an unsecured connection around the fourth floor – thank you, World of Warcraft Druid 386, whoever you are. Anyway, I finally got connected and that reference study that we're supposed to analyze ain't even online. It's only in some textbook."

Big shrugged. "So we do it old-school. We go to the library."

"Yeah, thanks. I thought of that, believe it or not," Chip quipped. "But the library is locked up tight and we can't get in. Looks like it'll have to wait."

Big looked surprised. "That's it?" he said.

"That's it what?" Chip replied.

"That's the best you can come up with?" Big smiled. "Chip, you're letting me down. I was expecting space aliens and volcanic eruptions and all you came up with is a locked door." With that, Big pushed his chair away from the table and started walking toward the hallway.

"Where are you going?" Chip called.

"I'm getting us into the library," Big called over his shoulder. "See you there shortly."

The table was quiet when a joyful Morrison waltzed back. He was grinning like a fool and walking on air.

"Well?" Trevor asked.

"She likes me," Morrison giggled.

"Really?" Trevor replied, leaning forward and anticipating the details.

"No, not really," Morrison said, losing his smile and shaking his head. "In fact, I'd say that there is bread mold that this girl would go out with before me."

"So there's hope for Langdon," Chip quipped.

"Shut up, Carson," Langdon snapped. "You see, that's exactly the kind of thing I'm talking about."

"So sorry," Chip replied sarcastically. "It's a reflex."

5 ONE HUNDRED PERCENT LANGDON-FREE

In the dimly lit upstairs hallway of Queen Elizabeth High School, Matt "Big" McMann was looking for the library. Through the maze of corridors, the tall boy wandered, hoping to stumble upon the magical room which would help him solve his academic woes.

It wasn't a complicated project he had been given, just a regular mid-term assignment. Unfortunately, he had been stuck with Chip as a lab partner. Big liked his fellow teammate a lot, but the laid-back Chip did not score high marks in the dependability department. After bugging Chip all week for his section of the report, the red-haired prankster had finally delivered a stack of blank paper, claiming that the project was done, but his printer was using invisible ink.

Now the project was due on Monday. If Big did not have it completed, his eight-year streak of straight A's would be out the window.

Turning a tight corner, Big squinted in the dim fluorescent lighting. At the far end of the hallway, Big spotted what he was looking for. Breaking into a jog, Big's heart fell into his sneakers as he noticed the doors were closed and the lights were dim in the QEH library. Big stretched out a meaty hand and gave the door handle a sharp tug. Much to his surprise, the door swung wide open.

Big was in the library.

"Too easy," the large boy mumbled, as he strode past the rows of computer terminals and racks of magazines that flanked the doors of the library.

Amongst the rows and rows of books, Big took a deep breath. Although he would never admit it, being both brainy and brawny, Big felt more at home in a library than he did on the basketball court.

Prowling the shelves, Big searched for the one book he needed to finish his project. Fortunately, there was only a small part of the project to be completed. Big had wisely not trusted Chip to do any of the complicated observations.

Big turned down a long aisle and started scanning the top shelf. All he needed was some information from a few pages in the biology book — a standard textbook, used in most Nova Scotia schools.

At the far end of the aisle, Big spotted what he was looking for.

"Aha!" cried Big, reaching out and grabbing the thick textbook.

"Hey!"

Big wheeled around to see a janitor barrelling down the aisle toward him.

"What do you think you're doing?"

Big tried to think fast. He was a horrible liar, so he figured the truth was his best option. "I was looking for a book so I could finish my biology project." Big held up the book for evidence.

"A likely story," the janitor shot back, almost running Big over with the large dust cart he was pushing. "You were looking to steal that book, weren't you?"

"No," Big replied.

"You were going to steal that book and then spray paint dirty words all over my clean walls, weren't you?"

"No, sir."

The janitor was much smaller than Big, with a round belly peeking out from under his shirt and a big moustache that was flecked with grey. His speech was like machine gun fire and he was waving his hands in the air.

"You were going to steal that book, spray paint dirty words all over my clean walls, and then glue the pages together on the big dictionary, weren't you?"

"No, sir."

"Well, not in my library you're not," the janitor cried. "Imagine a young feller's disappointment when he goes to look up a word in the dictionary and finds that all the D's have been glued together. It's happened before, you know. Imagine a dictionary with no D's.

You can't even spell dictionary without a D."

Big said nothing. It was obvious the janitor wasn't listening to him anyway.

"Now out you go!" the rough-looking man said finally. "Out, out, out!" With that, the janitor grabbed a broom from his dust cart and started sweeping Big toward the door.

"Okay, okay!" cried Big. "I'm going. You don't have to make my shoes all dusty."

"Out! And stay out of my library," the janitor jabbered. "You young hoodlums these days, always getting into trouble, breaking things, running in the streets . . ."

The janitor was still babbling as he swept Big right out of the doors and shut them firmly.

Big stared through the glass door a moment before the janitor shooed him away. The large boy let out a sigh. He knew his easy entry into the library had been too good to be true. He would have to come up with a plan.

★ ★ ★

"Three, two, one," cried Trevor. His "one" was punctuated by the sounding of the scoreboard buzzer. Trevor was standing on the sidelines of the basketball court. He and his teammates were gathered to watch the three-point shootout.

In the shootout, each contestant had forty-five seconds to take twenty shots, four at each of five stations around the edge of the three-point arc. The three-point line is about twenty feet from the basket. When a shooter gets on a roll, it's pretty exciting to watch. Unfortunately, in this contest, it was pretty painful to witness.

The contest had started with ten shooters, but after the first round, the bricklayers had been sent to the showers and only the true shooters remained. Those true shooters included Chip, Langdon Strong, and a player from the Cartier Academy.

Chip and Langdon were dead even; four curse words and six dirty glares apiece. They had also both nailed ten of their twenty shots.

"Let threedom ring, Chip!" Trevor cheered from the sideline. The players gathered at mid-court to decide who was going to shoot first in the final round. Going first was not really a bad thing in the contest, because if you went first you got to set the standard for the other players. In this case, Chip Carson would be the lead shooter.

"What's gotten into him?" Big whispered to Trevor. Chip was always quick off the dribble and was a fairly good passer, but last season he had been notorious for his poor shooting. In fact, the other guys on the Bears often joked that they'd be undefeated if Chip would only hit his jumpers.

Trevor shrugged his shoulders. "I guess he's so ticked off at Langdon that he's making his shots."

Actually, the fact that he had a hot hand was no

surprise to Chip. He had spent all summer stroking jumpers at the playground and had even spent a couple of weeks at a basketball camp honing his mechanics. He knew that if he just kept his cool and kept his rhythm, he'd have no trouble icing the competition.

Chip flashed a smile at Trevor and Big on the sidelines. "Put two bucks down on me to win this puppy and put some champagne on ice," he called.

Trevor grinned. "Done and done," he replied. Trevor never needed to be encouraged to start a betting pool, especially when Chip was hardly expected to beat the odds. Ever the businessman, Trevor stood to drain his teammates' wallets if Chip continued to drain his jumpshots.

"Shooter ready?" called the referee, preparing to hand Chip the first ball.

"Let's go," growled Chip, narrowing his eyes and focusing on the orange rim twenty feet away.

The scoreboard buzzer sounded and the crowd, which had gathered to watch the shootout, started cheering.

Chip got off to a rough start.

Clang, clang, clang, clang.

Trevor matched each miss with a painful wince. Chip was oh-for-four and moving to the far elbow of the arc — his least favourite place from which to shoot.

Chip squared his feet and paused to wipe his hands on his jersey before attacking the next rack of basketballs. He knew what the problem was. Despite appearing pretty loose for the guys, the pressure was starting to get to him. Chip had never wanted to win a game as badly as he wanted to win this. His stomach was tighter than the cap on a child-proof aspirin bottle.

Chip took a deep breath as precious seconds ticked from the shot clock. Suddenly the stocky point guard started doing what he always did when he wanted to relax. He started to sing.

He didn't sing loudly, it was just a low mumbling hum as he continued shooting.

"Row, row, row, your boat . . ." Swish!

"Gently down the stream . . ." Swish!

"Merrily, merrily, merrily, merrily . . ." Clang! Whoops!

"Life is but a dream." Swish!

Chip had nailed three of four shots. As he danced over to the next shooting station, his singing grew a little louder, and his shooting got even hotter.

"Twinkle twinkle . . ." Swish!

"Little star . . ." Swish!

"How I wonder . . ." Swish!

"What you are." Swish!

The referee gave Chip a strange look. "Are you all right, son?" he asked quietly as Chip did the electric boogie over to the fourth rack of balls.

Chip only smiled. He was feeling good, he was feeling the rhythm. He was in The Zone.

"Baa baa black sheep, have you any wool?" howled

Chip, draining another three and now singing at the top of his lungs.

"Yes sir! Yes sir! Three bags full!" Swish!

"He's singing nursery rhymes!" Trevor laughed from the sideline. "He's a nut! It's all over now!" Trevor high-fived Big and in a flash the whole Bears team, with the exception of Langdon, along with most of the fans in the bleachers, were wailing along with Chip.

"One for my master and one for my dame!"

"And one for the little boy who lives down the lane!"

Chip's musical shooting spree struck a sour note, however, as he bricked his first two attempts at the final shooting station. It didn't matter. As he made his last shots, the crowd was singing and cheering louder with each one.

Finally, with just one second left on the clock, Chip fingered the final ball.

"Hey, Langdon," he called above the roar of the crowd. "This one's for you." With that, Chip squinted his eyes shut and blindly heaved up a prayer.

Nothing but net.

The crowd went nuts. Chip loved it. Waving his hands and practically doing handsprings to the sideline, he almost collided with a glaring Langdon Strong.

"You're just weird," Langdon spat through clenched teeth.

"Yeah," mused Chip with a smile. "But I'm a weirdo who just shot fourteen for twenty. Good luck."

"Nice shooting," said the Cartier Academy player as Chip took a seat on the bench. "Hope you don't start singing nursery rhymes when you play us."

"They'll never play us," wisecracked Chad from behind his teammate. "Those losers will be knocked out after their next game."

"Thanks for coming out, Cha," shot back Chip. "I'll give you a dollar if you pull your bottom lip over your head."

Back on the court, Langdon looked as rigid as a cement statue as he toed the three-point line and fiercely gripped the first ball.

He started shooting well, but after going three-for-four on the first shooting station, he fell apart, missing his next five shots. When all was said and done, the gym was as quiet as a piano recital hall, and Langdon had only made eight of twenty shots.

"Way to go, Chip," Trevor said, congratulating his friend. It looked as if Chip had the competition in the bag.

"Tough break, Langdon," Chip said, as the Bears' star player trudged his way back to the bench. "What happened, your ego get in your eyes?"

"Shut up, Carson," Langdon growled. "Everyone knows I'm twice the player you'll ever be."

"Maybe so," countered Chip with a smile, "but at least I'll be playing in our next game. Remember our deal?"

Langdon said nothing and stared laser beams at Chip.

If the two teammates hadn't been so busy jawing at each other, they would have noticed that out on the court, the Cartier Academy player was shooting like a machine gun.

After his mediocre performance in the earlier rounds, no one expected the third shooter to even be a factor, but now, after eight shots, he had nailed an amazing eight.

Trevor looked nervously at Chip's score posted on the scoreboard at the end of the gym, and then listened to the cheers from the crowds as the Cartier Academy player bagged another bucket.

"What's gotten into this guy?" Trevor mused aloud. "This is not good," he said woefully, as the Cartier Academy player aced another rack of balls.

"I know," Big replied. "Chip could lose this."

"Not only that," Trevor said, "but I had this guy in the pool at nine-to-one odds. If I had put my money down on him, I would have made a fortune."

Trevor was right. With four more shots still to go, the Cartier player had already beaten Chip's score. Chip had lost.

"Tough break," Trevor said coming over and taking a seat next to Chip.

"Indeed, *tres* crappy," concurred Chip, not sounding the least bit perturbed. "Let's go play some penny hockey."

"Why are you so happy?" Trevor was a little thrown off.

"Why shouldn't I be?" Chip said, explaining the obvious. "The next game the Cape Breton Grizzly Bears play will be one hundred percent Langdon-free."

6 TAKING OUT THE TRASH

"Well, that was very interesting," commented Big as the band of Grizzly Bears shuffled out of the gym to get changed for their next game.

"It wasn't too bad, huh?" mumbled Chip, unwrapping a chocolate bar and stuffing the whole thing in his mouth.

"What's that smell?" piped up Trevor, crinkling his nose as a strong odour wafted over the boys.

"Smells like Langdon's breath," cracked Chip, looking around for a garbage can to dispose of his candy bar wrapper.

"Real original, Carson," snapped Langdon, still in a bad mood after the three-point shooting competition. "Man, something is really rank."

"Who do we play next?" Big asked.

"QEH," Chip replied, waving his sticky wrapper in the air. "Anyone see a trash can?"

"They'll be tough, huh?" intoned Trevor. "Home team and all."

No one replied. Everyone already knew the answer. "What stinks so bad?"

"All right," Chip exclaimed, still clutching his piece of garbage. "If I don't find a trash can, I'm going to throw this wrapper on the floor and litter in this ever-so-beautiful educational facility."

Trevor threw open the door to the Grizzly Bears' dressing room. In a flash, he knew what smelled so awful and where Chip could get rid of his candy wrapper.

They had found the garbage cans.

Not one, not two, but clearly every trash can in the entire school had been piled into the Grizzly Bears' change room. In fact, with the large assortment of trash cans, garbage pails, dumpsters, and refuse bins, it was quite likely that there was not a garbage receptacle in a three block radius. They were all in the Bears' room.

As a finishing touch, the culprits had scrawled, "GRIZZLY BEARS STINK" across the blackboard.

"This sucks," groaned Trevor, surveying the scene with disgust.

"Who would want to do something like this?" cried Big, crossing the room to his gym bag and gingerly picking up a banana peel that had been stuffed into one of his sneakers.

"Gee, only every team at the tournament," countered Chip, shooing away a brave seagull that had landed on the window ledge, hungrily eying a packet of old

French fries in a nearby dumpster. "Come on, let's get this crap out of here."

"Hey, I'm not moving any trash," protested Langdon.

Chip's mind was overcome with wisecracks involving Langdon and trash. In fact, so many insults popped into his head simultaneously that Chip was amazingly left speechless.

Fortunately, Chip didn't have to say anything, because Big stepped in and pointed at a nearby half-empty garbage can.

"Move it, Langdon," he instructed. "Or I'll dump you in it, and throw you out, too."

Langdon started to help.

★ ★ ★

Just outside the door to the QEH cafeteria, Jim Morrison was pacing back and forth. He had a game in half an hour and was already late for the team meeting. He nervously patted his hair and smoothed the front of his khaki pants. He anxiously checked his watch and peeked into the cafeteria. It was now or never.

"Um, hi there," Morrison said, quickly stepping across the tile floor and sidling up to his dream girl.

"Oh be still my heart," Caitlin cried melodramatically. "It's my knight in shining armour come to whisk me away and take me to Never-Never Land."

"Um, how are you?" Morrison was usually much

smoother, but something about this girl just made him blow his cool.

"I'm fantastic," grumbled Caitlin, pulling on a purple spike of hair so that it stuck up a little more at the back of her head. "I do not want to be here. I do not want to be helping out at this tournament. I do not want to associate with anything that has to do with basketball — and that includes you. Sorry to sound negative, but this is a pretty bleak weekend for me."

"Sorry to hear it," Morrison, mumbled. "My name's Jim."

"So you said the last time you approached me in this lame manner."

"Sorry."

"No need to be sorry," Caitlin answered back. "After all, with all that we have in common, pretty much all we can talk about is your name."

"Well, what are you interested in?" Morrison made another brave attempt to lure Caitlin into conversation.

"You getting up and leaving would interest me greatly," she replied, unfazed.

"Seriously."

Caitlin sighed. "I love music."

"Cool," Jim Morrison nodded. "I play the guitar, and my favourite band is Phried Phish, but I also like Dr. Dentist and the Holy Molars."

"I mean real music," Caitlin said, turning up her little nose. "You know, the classics — Mozart, Chopin,

Tchaikovsky. I especially like to examine how harmony was used in different historical periods and to explore the uses of counterpoint in musical compositions."

"Oh," Jim Morrison said.

Caitlin rolled her eyes. "How insightful," she said finally. "Now, if you'll excuse me, I must go and start making punch for the dance tonight. I've been assigned to the refreshment table — so challenging. I hope I can handle it."

Morrison stared as the razor-sharp Caitlin strutted off.

"I think I'm in love," he mumbled.

★ ★ ★

"Just do your best, guys," Coach Kenny pleaded as the downcast Bears slumped around the room. "Remember that later tonight you can go to the school dance. We'll have some fun then. In the meantime, keep your chins up and roll with the punches. I'll see you out there in about twenty minutes."

As Coach Kenny walked from the room, the Bears collectively let out a low groan.

"I really like Coach Kenny," Trevor said slowly, "but he has to work on his pre-game pep talks."

"The man is a walking cliché," Big replied glumly.

"So, Taps, what are these guys like anyhow?" Chip called, shooting jumpshots with balled up sweat socks into a wastepaper basket.

Taps said nothing. He was busy reading the large tournament board posted at the far end of the room.

Deciphering the schedule of games for a double-elimination tournament was a bit like following a road map of the New Jersey turnpike. For someone less knowledgeable than Taps, it would have been a cinch to get caught up in the tangle of lines, brackets, and consolation games. The Bears' bench-warmer followed it all through, however, as if he was reading a comic book.

"Something's not right," he said finally.

"I know something's not right," piped up Morrison, slipping back into the room, pleased that Coach Kenny wasn't around. "We're about to get creamed."

"No, something's wrong with the tournament brackets," replied Taps, calling the guys over to gather around the board. "Here we are, about to play the home team, right?" Taps pointed to jumble of lines and pairings on the board. "Since we lost our first game, we should be on the losing side of the bracket."

Big shrugged his enormous shoulders. "So?" The Bears' big man could explain complex physics equations, but even he was confused by the setup of a ten team, double-knockout tournament.

"Look here," Taps said. "According to this chart, the winner of this game gets to go straight into the finals!"

"How did that happen?"

"Who cares?" cried Chip. "Do you guys know what this means?"

"It means that the home team rigged the brackets to get an easy ride to the finals?" said Trevor.

"No!" shouted Chip. "It means that this is our chance. This is our one shot to show everyone that we're for real. Think about it; if we can just squeak out one win, there'll be no more pranks, no more wise-cracks, no more jokes about us. Everyone will have to take us seriously. This is great!"

The rest of the Grizzly Bears fell silent for a moment, imagining what would happen if they actually won.

Chip hopped up on a chair. "Let's pull it together guys, just for this one game. Let's make like a real team out there for once and show them that we're not a joke. All we have to do is win one game and we're in the finals!"

"So what?" Langdon sneered. "We couldn't win one game all year, why should we start now?"

"Because you weren't on the injured list all year, now you are," countered Chip, subtly reminding Langdon about the deal they had made before the three-point shootout. "Remember?"

"There's nothing wrong with me," Langdon re-torted. "I'll see you losers on the court." The Bears' super-ego stormed from the room.

As Langdon slammed the door, a low grumble swept through the room. In that instant, dreams of victory and success crumbled and the team returned to being the group of basketball bozos that they were so used to feeling like.

Chip sighed and shook his head. "He's not very good for team spirit, is he?"

At the back of the room, Big sullenly sat at a school desk. The tall boy stared into space as his teammates drifted out of the room.

"Hey, Big," called Chip, seeing his distraught friend. "Don't worry, buddy. We'll beat these guys. You'll see."

Big scowled. "I'm not worried about that, Chip. I'm worried about my — *our* — biology project."

"Oh," Chip waved his hand dismissively. "That." Big had told Chip about his trouble getting into the library and Chip had taken action in his typical manner. "You want to get into the library, right?"

Big nodded. "Unless you know another way to get information on DNA structure."

Chip let the remark slide. "Don't worry, Big. I've done some thinking and I've got a plan." Chip rummaged around in his red duffel bag and produced a sheet of paper. "Look, here's a diagram of the school's air conditioning system," he continued, shoving the piece of paper at Big. "You boost me up and I'll climb through an air vent in the ceiling. According to my map, there's exactly ninety-four feet of ventilation ducts I'll have to crawl through before I'm directly over the library. Then I'll pop out the air grate, jump down, open the door for you, and presto! *Bienvenue a la bibliothèque!*" Chip beamed. "Simple, huh?"

Big furrowed his brow. "How did you get blueprints to the air vent system?"

Chip lost his smile. "I didn't, exactly. But it looks right, doesn't it?"

Big squinted his eyes and sighed. "Maybe a teacher is around," he said quietly, getting up and trudging out of the classroom.

"Big!" called Chip, holding up his map. "Are you in, or what? Let's do this, man!"

Big waved for his overzealous biology partner to follow him and walked out the door. Climbing the stairs to the second floor of the school, Big mulled over his options. If he could find a teacher, perhaps he could smooth talk his way into the library; if not — Big glanced at his blissful teammate walking beside him — there was no way he was going to let Chip crawl through ventilation ducts.

Turning the corner, the boys were surprised at what they saw. Not only were the doors to the library wide open, but the lights were on and a librarian was sitting at the front desk.

Rubbing his eyes, Big wondered if he was seeing a mirage. He couldn't believe his good fortune.

"See, what did I tell you?" Chip said casually. "I told you I had a plan."

"Silence," Big said gruffly. He was carefully

rehearsing exactly what he was going to say.

"Excuse me, sir," Big said cautiously as he approached the librarian.

"Yes?" the man replied, looking up from the stack of papers he was marking. He was a small man, with grey hair and a thin, grey beard. He wore a checkered shirt with the sleeves rolled up and a pair of steel-rimmed spectacles that kept slipping down to the end of his nose. He looked like the kind of man who smoked a pipe.

"Um, would you mind if we came in to do some research for our biology project?" Big asked tentatively.

"Well, by all means. I only opened the door because Stanley wanted some extra study time," the librarian replied with a smile, pointing to a short, pudgy boy sitting at a round table in the middle of the room. "If you need to do some work too, please feel free to join us."

"Too easy," Chip cried as the two walked away. "I can't believe you were complaining about this."

Big grinned as he made a beeline to the shelf where, earlier, he had found the biology textbook he needed.

Scanning the shelf, Big's smile quickly faded. Every book was exactly where it had been before, with the exception of the thick textbook. Big's heart fell when he saw a gap on the shelf where the textbook used to be.

Turning around, Big started to head back to the front desk to inquire on the whereabouts of the book.

"It was here an hour ago," he called to Chip.

"Shhhh," hissed Stanley from his study area in the middle of the library. "I'm trying to get some work done over here."

"Sorry," Big muttered, looking over at the short boy who was surrounded by stacks of books. "Hey!" On the table in front of Stanley was the textbook Big needed. "Where did you get that textbook?"

Stanley raised his head and gestured at the rows and rows of bookshelves. "Take a guess," he said shortly, it was clear he did not want to be disturbed.

"Do you mind if we borrow it?" Big said, trying not to sound desperate.

The pudgy pupil looked up at the towering Big. Stanley's unruly mat of curly black hair hung over his forehead, half-concealing his acne. There was nothing, however, to conceal the expression of irritation on Stanley's face.

"Certainly," Stanley said, with about as much politeness as he could manage without throwing up. "You may borrow this book . . . when I am finished with it." The boy then resumed his reading.

"Looks like someone took their grumpy pills this morning," Chip said, taking a seat directly beside the studying Stanley.

Big nervously paced around the empty library as Chip sat perfectly still about half a foot from Stanley. The red-haired boy stared at Stanley as the poor student tried to continue his reading. Finally, the pudgy boy couldn't take it any more.

"What are you doing?" he demanded, turning his head and almost rubbing noses with Chip.

"Waiting."

"Waiting?"

"Waiting for you to finish," Chip said matter-of-factly.

"Fine," Stanley snapped. "Wait." With that, Stanley resumed his reading. Chip had never seen anyone read angrily before, but he found it fascinating to watch. As a result, Chip stared at Stanley while Big stared at the clock and the minutes passed like hours.

The stony silence was broken only by the sound of Stanley slowly flipping the pages of the book.

After about five minutes of awkward silence, Big couldn't keep quiet any longer. "Um, excuse me."

Stanley painfully raised his eyebrows expectantly.

"Um, *when* will you be finished with that?" Big asked, glancing nervously at the textbook. The Bears did have a game soon and he really needed to take some notes.

Stanley slowly turned his head again and glared at the clock, then he glared at Big. "I will be finished," he growled slowly, "Monday."

"That's when Stanley writes his test," piped in the librarian, trying to be neighbourly and smooth over the fact that this Stanley guy was being about as pleasant as a porcupine in a sleeping bag.

"Yes, my test," Stanley said pointedly. "The one I am currently trying to study for. Now, if you'll excuse me."

Big nervously clicked his tongue.

There was another moment of silence before Chip spoke.

"I'm afraid Monday is no good for us. How about giving us the book now?"

"I don't care!" Stanley cried. "I found it first, so deal with it!"

"Pipe down, boys," the librarian shushed. Even in an empty library he wasn't about to let the boys shout.

"Okay," Big pleaded. "I'll give you a bag of chips if you give us the book."

Stanley looked at Big like he was crazy.

"A bag of chips and a pack of gum," Chip added.

Stanley rolled his eyes. "Forget it."

"Okay," Chip tried again. "I'll make you a deal."

Interrupted once more, Stanley sighed and stared laser beams at Chip.

"I'm thinking of a number between one and one hundred," Chip continued, unfazed. "If you guess the number, you give us the book. If you don't guess the number, I take the book from you. Deal?"

"I already have the book," Stanley hissed, trying to control his temper. "What type of a stupid deal is that?"

"It's a good deal!" cried Chip. "It's a good deal for us!"

"We really need to see that textbook," Big added.

"Look," Stanley cried, hopping out of his seat and standing toe-to-toe with the towering Big. "I am trying to study. Now, if you two freaks would leave me alone I might be able to finish. I am not about to just hand over this book because you bonehead jocks are trying to muscle it out of me. I need to study. Now please go away."

Stanley looked like a puffed-up poodle squaring off with a pit bull as he stood up to Big. The small boy was looking Big squarely in the stomach while he told him off. Despite looking ridiculous, Stanley had gotten his point across.

"Fine," Big said meekly, as he plodded out of the library. "We'll be back later."

"You really need to teach that guy some people skills," Chip commented to the librarian as he followed Big out the door. "He definitely does not work or play well with others."

Big was downcast as he walked with Chip toward the stairs. Twice he had almost been able to complete his project and twice he had been denied. Talk about being born under a bad sign.

Chip suddenly clapped his hands to bring Big out of his funk. "All right," the shorter boy cried, excitedly. "I've got a plan. All we need is a stun gun, fishing net, four waterproof matches, and a —"

"Cut it, Chip," Big said seriously. "We've got to get

this done and we're going to do it my way. There is no way I'm taking an incomplete on this project."

★ ★ ★

Playing against the home team is never easy. It is quite intimidating when everyone in the gymnasium is rooting for the other team.

The Grizzly Bears knew this as soon as they stepped onto the court, to a loud chorus of boos.

"Geez, what did we do to deserve this?" grumbled Big, still in a bad mood from his run-in with Stanley in the library.

"We showed up," replied Trevor.

The Grizzly Bears ran through their warm-ups, all the while trying not to look at their opponents on the other end of court.

The QEH Lions had always been a strong team. They were infamous for their size and their ability to overpower opponents. This year was no exception, as it looked as if all but two of their players stood over six feet tall.

"What do they put in the water in this town?" wondered Trevor, nailing a jumpshot from about twenty feet out.

"Fertilizer," answered Chip as he made his way over to Langdon who was stretching out on the floor. "Remember our deal," he said. "Tell the Coach you're hurt."

Langdon looked at Chip as if he were crazy. "Go slam your head in a door," Langdon spat, lumbering to his feet and strutting away.

"That went well," Chip mumbled.

Back on the bench, Coach Kenny was finishing up another half-hearted pep talk. "All right, guys, here we go," he cried as he rhymed off the regular Bears starters. "Let's play tough out there, fellas."

Right from the opening tipoff, Chip knew it was going to be a usual Bears blowout. QEH fast-breaked down the court and were up by a bucket before Big was even sure which way the Grizzly Bears were shooting.

In the meantime, Langdon took the inbound pass and was busy streaking down the court. He had tossed up an off-balance three-pointer before his teammates had even crossed the half-court line.

The QEH front line was destroying the Grizzly Bears' defence. Time after time they marched down the court like a big blue wave, hammering the Grizzly Bears with their superior size and scoring at will.

At halftime, the lights on the QEH side of the scoreboard were practically burned out. The Grizzly Bears were down by fifteen.

Halftime was awkward. Coach Kenny spent most of the ten-minute break begging the guys not to embarrass themselves. Langdon spent his time complaining about pretty much everyone on the team. And Morrison spent his time writing a love poem, which he planned to give to Caitlin Burrack.

"Hey Trevor," Morrison called across the crowded room. "What rhymes with 'bellybutton ring'?"

"Shut up, Morrison."

By the time they took the court for the second half warm-up, team morale was not exactly soaring.

"Only another fifteen minutes, and then we're done, huh?" Trevor observed, dropping in a jumpshot from the top of the key.

"Don't look at it like that," Chip replied. "Let's at least give them a game."

"Whatever," Trevor rolled his eyes and nailed another jumper.

"Trevor, why don't you shoot like that in a game?"

"I don't know," Trevor answered. "I guess I just never get the ball."

"I bet you can't shoot like that in a game," Chip said matter-of-factly.

Trevor bristled at the word 'bet.' "Sure I can."

"Okay, I bet you five bucks you can't hit five jump-shots in the second half."

Trevor swished another jumper. "Deal," he said quickly.

Chip turned away so his friend wouldn't see him smiling.

The buzzer sounded and both teams trotted onto the court.

"Hey guys, huddle up," cried Chip, wanting to talk

to his teammates without Coach Kenny hearing what he had to say.

Chip's teammates — with the exception of Langdon — crowded around their point guard. "Don't forget that this is our one chance to get some respect. I have as much fun on this team as anyone, but I think that it might be even more fun if we actually won a game "

The other players nodded in agreement.

"Let's play like a team for once," Chip continued. "Especially since Langdon's not playing."

"What are you talking about?" Big replied. "He's right over there."

"He doesn't have to not play to not play," replied Chip meaningfully. "We're only going to win if everyone is involved. Got it, guys?" Chip gave his teammates a hard stare.

"We get it, Chip," replied Trevor. "But one more thing," he added with a smile. "Would you relax? You make me nervous when you're not clowning around."

Chip grinned and let out a big cheer. "Let's pluck these turkeys!"

With a sharp tweet of the whistle, the referee signalled the start of the second half.

Big passed the ball to Chip in the backcourt. The stocky point guard had barely bounced the ball once when Langdon Strong raced over, hands outstretched, expecting to take possession.

Instead of handing the ball to Langdon, Chip fired a

bullet pass to a streaking Trevor at mid-court.

Trevor bounced the ball twice and proceeded to ice an eighteen-foot jumper.

"That's one," Trevor smiled as he passed Chip on the way back downcourt. "I hope you got that five bucks on you."

"Defence, Trevor," Chip replied. "I got ball."

Some coaches say that defence is ten percent the ability to stop your opponent, and ninety percent the desire to do it. If that is the case, then it was no surprise that Chip seemed to be in total overdrive as he shuffled alongside of the QEH point guard, cutting him off and driving him to his weak side.

Seeing Chip had his man along the sideline, Trevor raced up to really put on the pressure.

He came up too soon, however, and the QEH guard lobbed an easy pass to the now-open man, who raced in and scored the layup.

"Aw, come on, Trevor," complained Langdon. "Let's not be stupid."

"Cut the crap, Langdon," Chip said, taking the in-bounds pass from Big and racing upcourt.

"Shut up and give me the ball, Carson."

"Not a chance."

Chip paused at the top of the key, surveying the defence and looking to make something happen.

In the low post, Big was battling with the centre of the opposing team. After much scuffling, Big managed to get the QEH player neatly pinned on his hip and was wildly calling for the ball.

Chip dumped a little shovel pass to Big and, instead of standing still, proceeded to cut through the key. Big saw him and connected on a little behind-his-back pass which Chip converted into a layup.

"Good give-and-go!" shouted Morrison from the bench.

But the Lions weren't about to quit. They came down the court, attacking the Grizzly Bears' defence, zipping the ball from player to player, hardly ever taking more than a dribble before passing it off, always looking for a good shot.

The ball on the wing, a spindly forward crouched and waited as the QEH centre rushed up to set a screen on Trevor.

"Pick right!" hollered Chip, but the warning was too late. Trevor was bumped off and the QEH player was already zooming toward the hoop.

Big saw the open lane, and came over to help out. The large boy set his feet and threw his hands straight up, making him seem the size of a small bungalow. The QEH player wasn't about to slow down, however, and he took two giant steps and launched himself right into Big's broad chest.

Tweet!

The referee stopped the play to call a foul.

Big's mouth dropped open and Chip was already

hurrying toward the referee to protest the call.

"Offensive foul, number seventeen blue," the referee shouted at the scorers' table.

"*Offensive* foul?" yelled Chip, high-fiving Big. "Did I hear that right? Did we actually get a call in our favour?"

Big slapped hands with the rest of the guys on the floor. When the Grizzly Bears got a favourable call, it was a rare day indeed.

On the bench, Coach Kenny was a bit confused. Six minutes into the second half and his team had cut the lead to nine, but Langdon had yet to take a shot. He was perplexed as to why his star player wasn't involved in the offence. Coach Kenny turned to say something to Morrison, but then decided just to keep quiet.

On the court, the Grizzly Bears were working the ball around the perimeter of the defence. Finally, Chip fired a bounce pass to Big in the post, who immediately touch-passed it to Trevor, who was spotting up on the wing.

Trevor quickly checked his feet to confirm that he was behind the three-point stripe and squared his shoulders to the hoop.

"No, Trevor!" shouted Coach Kenny, seeing that Trevor was about to shoot. "No threes. Pass it off, pass it off!" Trevor launched the shot. "No, no, no," cried the coach, covering his eyes, but peeking through a crack in his fingers. The ball ripped through the nylon mesh. "Good shot, Trevor!" Coach Kenny cheered. "Way to go!"

Morrison shot Coach Kenny a look.

"What?" the young coach shrugged awkwardly.

On the court, Langdon was shouting at every one of his teammates. "Give me the ball, you losers!" he yelled, oblivious to the fact that the Grizzly Bears were actually cutting into QEH's lead. "Carson, I'll get you for this!"

Finally, Langdon had had enough. On the next play down the court, Chip was patiently dribbling the ball on the wing, waiting for Trevor to set a screen for Big, when Langdon snuck behind him and stole the ball from his own teammate.

Coach Kenny wheeled to Morrison. "Did Langdon just do what I think he did?" he asked incredulously.

Morrison nodded silently. Coach Kenny shook his head and angrily thumbed for the first round of substitutions to come in off the bench. Jim Morrison and Davis O'Toole trotted in from the scorers' table.

When Chip saw his regular backup, Davis, he hung his head and made toward the bench.

"Hold up, Chip," called Davis. "I'm in for Langdon."

"What?" exploded Langdon. "Who says?"

"Um, the coach," Davis said, stating the obvious.

Langdon, on the verge of a fit, rushed over and started yelling at Coach Kenny.

"What are you, nuts?" he shouted. "What do you think you're doing?"

Coach Kenny looked around uneasily. Pretty much

the whole gym was watching the Bears player tear a strip off his coach.

"Take a seat, Langdon," Coach Kenny said, trying to assume authority.

"No way. I'm staying on the court," Langdon stuck his chin out defiantly.

Coach Kenny narrowed his eyes. "Park it, Strong!" he shouted, pointing at the pine. "Now." It was quite likely the first time that Coach Kenny had ever sincerely yelled at one of his players.

Langdon shot a glare at Coach Kenny that would have melted plastic. He also took a seat.

Chip looked on as a flustered Coach Kenny took a long swig on a water bottle and tried to calm down. "I think I love that man," he smiled.

Back on the court, the Grizzly Bears were experiencing something that they had never experienced before — a comeback. With only two minutes to go, they were only down by three points. The score was the Cape Breton High School Grizzly Bears forty, the shocked, stunned, and confused Queen Elizabeth High School Lions forty-three.

With time running out, Coach Kenny was really at a loss. Usually by this point in the game, his team was so far behind that he could just sit back and relax. Now, he was still on his feet barking instructions at any player who would listen.

"Langdon, get in there," he barked as a whistle blew

to signal substitutions. No one moved on the bench. "Langdon!" he repeated.

"Um, Coach, Langdon left," Taps piped in from the end of the bench.

"Left?" Coach Kenny repeated in disbelief.

Taps shrugged and pointed to the door. "You want me to go in instead?" the thin boy asked hopefully.

"Maybe in a minute," Coach Kenny replied.

"But there's only a minute left, Coach." Taps wouldn't let it rest.

"Exactly." Coach Kenny called for a time out.

"All right, guys," he began nervously. Every eye was on him and Coach Kenny was not sure how to lead his team to victory. "There's only a minute and a half left, so we're going to have to hurry here. Let's put some tough, man-to-man defence on them and when we get the ball back, call time out so we can set up our last play."

"All right, Coach," cried Chip, throwing his hand in the middle of the huddle. "Bears on three . . . One, two, three!"

"*Bears!*" shouted the entire team.

As soon as the five players got back onto the court, Chip called them together for a quick huddle of their own.

"All right, guys, we've got a ton of time here. Let's start off with a one-three-one full court press."

"But Coach said —"

"Trust me. Start with a one-three-one press. And no one call a time out because we don't have any left. Let's hold for the last shot, set lots of screens, and look for Big down low."

As Trevor took his position for the press, Chip called over to him. "What's up? You look worried."

Trevor nodded. "Only a minute left, and I've only hit four jumpers. If I don't score, I'll owe you five bucks."

Chip smiled.

The referee blew the whistle to begin play.

The QEH Lions were a little nervous. All the pressure was now on them. Everyone had expected them to bury the Grizzly Bears. The crowd had sat in shocked silence since the beginning of the second half. Now it looked like the players were a little edgy as well.

QEH had to inbound the ball from under their own hoop. Chip was playing so close to the QEH point guard that he could tell what the guy ate for lunch. Finally, the QEH big man managed to inbound the ball to the other guard.

Chip and Trevor promptly converged and smothered the player hard against the sideline. The QEH player flipped a weak pass over to mid-court, where it flew just over Jim Morrison's outstretched hands. One more pass and the ball was with the QEH forward who had parked himself under the Grizzly Bears' basket. The QEH Lions had successfully cracked the Grizzly Bears' full-court press.

Big was supposed to be guarding the basket, but found himself out of position. QEH had a clear shot at the basket with time winding down.

The lanky QEH player bounced the ball twice and powered himself in for a layup.

Pressure does weird things to a person, however, and while it was an easy shot, the ball bounced painfully around the cylinder before trickling off the far edge of the rim and right into Big's meaty hands.

The Grizzly Bears still had a chance.

The clock was ticking and fifteen seconds were all that remained.

With the power of a piston engine, Big fired the ball to Jim Morrison on the far sidelines. Morrison spun around and zipped a pass to Chip.

Chip bounced the ball between his legs and squinted at the time remaining. The Bears needed a three pointer and that would only be for the tie. Chip sized up the situation. On his right, Morrison was battling for position in the low post, on the other side, Big had just set a screen for Trevor who was popping out to the three-point line on the baseline. He was being closely trailed by a QEH defender.

Chip fired a pass over to Trevor who took a little hop step and launched a rainbow from the deep corner. The ball had just left Trevor's hand when he was pummelled by the QEH player and fell to the floor in a heap.

The next three events happened almost simultaneously. The referee blew his whistle for a foul, the final buzzer sounded, and Trevor's shot found the bottom of the net.

The gym was totally silent.

Chip rushed over to see if his friend was all right.

"Did it . . . go?" Trevor said quietly, the wind knocked out of him.

"Nothing but net," Chip cried. "And the foul!"

"You owe me five," smiled Trevor.

"Get up, you clown," Chip said, dragging Trevor to his feet with Big's help.

Still a little winded, Trevor took a deep breath to clear his head. He slowly began making his way to the foul. Trevor had a chance for a four-point play. The rarest play in basketball.

There was no time left on the clock and the score was tied. If Trevor made his one foul shot, the Grizzly Bears would have won their first game in recent history.

"Betcha you miss," cried a voice in the bleachers.

Trevor wheeled around. "Who said that?"

"I did," called a fat boy in a ball cap in the front row. "Two bucks, you miss."

"On," Trevor replied. "Anyone else?"

"I've got five that you brick it," yelled a student with a bad goatee.

"On," Trevor replied, going over to the crowd to shake on the bet. By the time Trevor worked his way down the line he stood to win or lose about twenty bucks depending on whether he made the shot.

"Hey, Chip," he said, toeing the foul line. "If I miss this, you're buying me lunch."

"And if you make it?"

"I'll buy the champagne."

With no time left on the clock, no players were allowed to line up along the key. It was just Trevor, the hoop, and over a hundred booing QEH fans.

Trevor bounced the ball twice and calmly stroked a clean foul shot.

The Bears had won.

7 ROCK AND ROLL FOREVER

After their victory against the home team Lions, the Bears couldn't wait to party. Back at their hotel, most of the team crowded into Chip's tiny room to talk about the game.

"I still can't believe we won," cried Taps fixing his glasses and pouring another glass of soda pop. "Their numbers were higher than ours in nine of ten major statistical categories."

"Which category were we higher in?"

"Turnovers."

Everyone in the room started laughing, with the exception of Chip. The Bears' point guard had his headphones plugged in and was staring at the TV with a huge grin etched on his face.

"Hey, Chip," shouted Big from across the room. "How do you hear the TV with your headphones on?"

Chip perked up and lazily rolled his head to one side. "I don't, Big," he replied simply. "I just watch the shows and make up my own dialogue. Now if you'll excuse me, I must get back to the high-tension action-drama I'm watching."

Big glanced at the TV and then back to Chip. "That's a cartoon, Chip!"

"Use your imagination," Chip smiled.

The only one in the room not in high spirits was Morrison. He was slumped in a corner chair, absently picking at his guitar.

"Do you think Caitlin Burrack would like me if I wrote her a song?" he asked no one in particular.

"Sure," replied Trevor. "If the song was 'Hit The Road, Jack.'"

"Or maybe 'Jump For My Love.'" laughed Big. "But only if you sing it on the balcony."

"Oh, you guys are a regular laugh riot," replied Morrison. "If only you knew how much my heart was aching."

"If only you knew how much my head was aching from you yapping about this freaky girl," shot back Trevor. "Face it, Morrison, the only reason you're interested in that spiky-haired weirdo is because she's not the least bit interested in you."

"It *is* a little refreshing," Morrison admitted. "Anyway, if you'll excuse me, I have to compose a song that will melt her heart."

"I've seen the way she looks at you," replied Big, grabbing the remote control from Chip and turning up the volume on the TV. "You couldn't melt her heart with a blowtorch."

"Hey!" cried Chip, peeling his headphones off and getting ready to wrestle with Big for the remote. Chip took one look at the bulky boy and came to his senses.

"Get ready, you guys," instructed Trevor. "We've got to go soon."

Taps nervously poked at his thick glasses. "Are we really going to this dance thing?"

Morrison bobbed his head enthusiastically. "Are you kidding? We're a championship-calibre basketball team. The women are going to be wild about us!"

"Yeah, right," scoffed Big. "I'm sure they're going to be especially impressed that we fluked out and beat their home team. We are going to be about as popular as a three-week-old baloney sandwich."

"Maybe we should just stay here and play video games," Taps suggested eagerly.

A few of the Grizzly Bears mumbled their agreement. Most of them shied away from dances back home. This one would have only strangers in attendance. Finally, Chip had had enough.

"Okay, guys," Chip cried, jumping off the bed and pulling down the hood of his sweatshirt. "Get back to your rooms. We're meeting back here in half an hour. Now don't be a bunch of dolts. We're winners tonight, and winners don't sit at home and play video games when there's a party right across the street. Besides, I want to party and I'm not going by myself." He paused long enough to do a perfect three-step spin-move in the middle of the floor. "Now go to your rooms and put some nice clothes on, comb your hair, and take a shower — not necessarily in that order — and then we're going to paint this town beige, baby!"

"That's red, Chip," Trevor corrected. "Paint the town red."

Chip tried to look hurt. "I'm colour-blind, Trevor," he sniffled. "And I'm a little sensitive about it, if you don't mind. Now let's go!"

Trevor grinned and turned to the rest of the guys. "Let's go," he repeated.

In exactly thirty minutes, the Cape Breton Grizzly Bears reassembled in Chip's room. It was hard to recognize the guys. With the help of a little soap and some cheap cologne, they had transformed from a collection of ruddy, perspiration-caked jocks into mini-models straight from the pages of GQ *Magazine*.

Except for Chip.

Chip Carson was still dressed in the same red hooded sweatshirt and grey nylon trackpants that he had had on when he delivered his inspired party pep talk.

"What happened to you?" asked Big, fixing the collar of his shirt.

"I kind of fell asleep," confessed Chip, running his fingers through his messier-than-usual red hair.

"Are you still coming?"

"What? You think I'm going to bail, just 'cause I

don't look like I stepped from the pages of a fashion magazine?" Chip pulled a ball cap low over his eyes. "Puh-leaze!" He did a few Justin Timberlake-esque dance moves and high-fived Trevor. "Let's party!"

★ ★ ★

Looking at the QEH gymnasium, no one would have suspected that any basketball games had taken place a mere four hours ago.

At both ends of the gym, the large glass backboards were cranked up so they faced the ceiling. The hoops which sprouted from the walls were draped with streamers and balloons. A small DJ booth was set up at the far end of the gym, right beside a makeshift stage where a band would be performing later. There were punch and candy bars laid out on what used to be the scorers' table, and a large disco ball dangled from the middle of the gym, completing the setup for the dance.

The dance wasn't exclusively for the basketball teams in town for the tournament. It was a regular QEH school dance, which the visiting teams were invited to attend. As a result, the dance floor was packed and there was a long lineup of people waiting to be let in.

QEH students were jammed into the front entrance of the school, with a few basketball players towering above the milling crowd. Overdressed teachers in suits and gowns acted as chaperones, standing behind the front table while two volunteers collected admission to the dance.

Beside the front table, Caitlin Burrack's personal nightmare continued. As part of her school-spirit-building punishment, she had been assigned to look after the coat check and refreshment table for the dance.

Caitlin grabbed another coat and pitched it onto the pile that served as the "coat check." In another couple of hours, she would be free of her extra-curricular parade of punishments and she could get back to being herself. The sooner she got away from the hoopla of the basketball tournament the better. She had already decided to spend the next day sipping cafe lattes at her favourite coffee shop on Spring Garden Road, far away from anything that might contribute to school spirit.

"Hey, Caitlin."

The glum girl was plucked from her daydream by the cheery greeting from Jim Morrison.

"Oh, hello," she gave him a sickly-sweet grin.

"You working the door?" Morrison stated the obvious.

"No, I'm doing a forensic investigation for the RCMP," Caitlin snarled through clenched teeth, grabbing Morrison's jean jacket and giving it an unceremonious toss over her shoulder. "Ticket," she growled, shoving a coat check tag into his hand.

"Er, thanks," Morrison gave her a long look and shuffled nervously. "Listen, um, maybe later you can save me a dance?"

"Sure," Caitlin replied icily. "With who?"

"Ouch," Trevor winced and pushed a dazed Morrison past the coat check table and into the gym. Caitlin watched them go, a small smile cracking through her deep purple lipstick

"Hey, Morrison," Big teased as the group of boys wandered into the gym. "She really likes you."

Morrison gave Big a blank stare and shrugged. Entering the gym, the boys were blasted by the vicious volume of the pounding dance music filling the gym.

"Hey, Chip," yelled Trevor. "Did you really have to bring your gym bag?"

Chip gave Trevor a look and adjusted the strap of his duffel bag. "Indeed I did," he replied as coolly as possible while shouting at the top of his lungs. "I wanted to look good, so I brought extra cologne, hair mousse, talcum powder, conditioning gel, dental floss, a mud mask, and a pedicure kit."

"Chip, you don't use any of that stuff," Trevor shouted. "You don't even use a comb!"

Chip shrugged. "Always be prepared — that's my motto."

The group of Grizzly Bears quickly scouted out the gymnasium before setting up camp in a small circle of chairs along the same wall as the refreshment table. Out on the dance floor, clusters of students started moving with the rhythm of the music that pounded out of four large speakers set beside the DJ booth.

Bridging the gap between the DJ booth and the refreshment table was a low stage. On the riser, long-haired roadies were working to tape down cords, set up the drum kit, and plug in amplifiers to get ready for the live band that was performing later that evening.

Not having anyone to dance with, nor the inclination to find someone to dance with, the Bears simply reclined in their chairs and surveyed the scene. Besides, everyone was still riding high from the day's victory. Even though no one paid them any special attention, they felt like they were kings.

Looking cool at a high school dance was an art that Jim Morrison had long since mastered. With his casual white T-shirt and hair that was neat enough to be presentable but messy enough to show that he was too cool to care about it, Morrison positively dripped attitude. He was also visibly flustered when Caitlin Burrack approached him as the DJ played the first slow song of the night.

"Are you going to dance, or what?" Caitlin cried over the blare of the ballad.

Morrison couldn't have popped off his chair faster if it had been spring-loaded. "Sure," he stammered.

"Good," replied Caitlin slyly. "Then you won't mind if I take your chair." With that, Caitlin tweaked her nose ring and hauled Morrison's chair off toward the refreshment table.

Even over the din of the music, the Bears' laughter could be heard loud and clear. Morrison, realizing he had been sucked in, casually leaned against the wall and desperately tried to resume his air of cool. Somehow, however, the effect had been shattered.

The Bears were wallflowers. They preferred to stare at people dancing rather than get out on the floor themselves. In fact, Taps grew so disinterested that he dug a piece of paper from his pocket and started going over the statistics of the next day's opposing team.

"Cartier Academy," he shouted in Chip's ear, waving their team stat sheet in the air. "They already annihilated us by forty-four earlier this year and —"

"Thanks, Taps." Chip didn't need to be reminded of the humiliating loss earlier that season. He snatched the paper and quickly scanned the statistics. Their numbers were so good that Chip wondered if Cartier Academy would soon be named a new NBA franchise.

"No problem, guys," Chip called, leaning forward in his chair. "Nobody expected us to make it this far. Let's win one more game and show everyone that we're the real deal. This is it, boys. This is the big time. Let's forget about how lousy we were then; let's remember how good we are now."

The Bears silently nodded their heads and narrowed their eyes. They actually looked confident.

"Do you really think we have a chance?" Trevor leaned over and yelled in Chip's ear.

Chip nodded his head enthusiastically. "Nope," he said flatly. "But don't tell them that."

Trevor smiled.

"I'm worried about Morrison," Chip continued, staring at the Bears' heartbroken heartthrob. "That femme fatale is really putting his stomach in the blender."

"Well, this should cheer him up," Trevor replied as a group of eight girls started to make their way over to where the Grizzly Bears were sitting. In the lead was a pretty blond girl.

"How does he do it?" Chip asked.

"Who knows?" Trevor replied. He had seen Morrison in action so many times that it was now a little boring. "Wanna go spit in the punch?" Trevor suggested, losing interest in Morrison and the group of descending females.

The girls had not gone unnoticed by Morrison, who was now back in full-blown cool mode.

"Nah," Chip declined. "We may as well watch in awe as Morrison works his magic."

But it was Morrison who was in awe as the girls brushed right by him before nestling beside a very stunned Taps.

"Hey there," the pretty girl said. "I'm Courtney."

"Hello," squeaked Taps in a strangled whisper, trying to fix his glasses and smooth his short black hair at the same time. He was not used to dealing with girls. In fact, as far as Taps was concerned, a date was a kind of fruit. "I'm Taps — I mean, William."

"Would you like to dance with us, William?" Courtney asked, flashing a small grin and giving Taps a double-dose of cute.

Taps looked nervously at the group of girls and tried to loosen his collar, which was already quite loose around his skinny neck. "Can they come?" he asked hesitantly, gesturing to the rest of the Bears.

Courtney quickly held a conference with her friends. Within moments, the Bears were out of their chairs and on the dance floor.

By this time in the evening, the DJ was long gone and a live band had taken to the makeshift stage. Phlegm, made up of three QEH students and one Dalhousie University dropout, was one of the trashiest garage bands in Halifax. They were wildly popular with the students and all of the teachers hated them, which made them that much more popular.

It was during Phlegm's most rowdy number, "Cockroach in the Cafeteria," that Jim Morrison wandered away from the group to grab another glass of orange punch from the refreshment table.

As the tall boy grabbed a paper cup, he noticed that Caitlin Burrack was slumped in her chair behind the table. Her nightmarish coat check duties complete, she had been reassigned to the refreshment table and, judging by the look on her face, she was equally thrilled with her new job.

Morrison drained his paper cup in one quick drink. The orange punch had a funny taste that made Morrison wince. "Nice punch," he lied.

Caitlin rolled her eyes. "Nice orange moustache," she replied, gesturing to his upper lip.

Morrison self-consciously wiped his lip until the remnants of the orange drink were well rubbed away.

"Do you like this band?" Morrison asked.

Caitlin sighed heavily and looked away.

Across the gym, Chip and Trevor were awkwardly shuffling to the music, while Taps danced with six or seven QEH girls.

"Would you look at that guy?" Chip was utterly amazed. "He can really cut a rug and those girls like him. I didn't think it was possible."

"I think Morrison could actually pick up some pointers from our new-found loverboy over there," Trevor agreed, watching as Taps concluded a song by dipping one of the girls.

"Speaking of Morrison," Chip cried. "Where did he get to?"

His question was answered as the music suddenly ended and the lead singer of Phlegm stepped into the spotlight.

"How are you losers doing tonight?" hissed a shaggy young man with large rings through his nose, ears, and eyebrows. An explosive cheer rose from the packed gymnasium. "As if we care," the lead singer continued, throwing his hands in the air and making a rude gesture to the crowd. The cheer grew even louder.

"Shut up!" commanded the Phlegm singer, trying to hide a smirk as the crowd ate up his bad-boy rock-star routine. "Now, I hate it when people make special requests and I hate it even more when you jerk-sticks out there think you can jam with us. 'Cause we rock and y'all suck."

He paused for another cheer.

"But! We've got a guy here tonight who we're going to make an exception for." Trevor and Chip exchanged a nervous look. "Let's give up for a guy from Cape Breton who wants to sing a special song for a special lady. How would you losers like to see . . . Jim . . . Morrison?!"

Like a group of seals, the crowd rocked the rafters with applause as Morrison sheepishly took to the stage.

"Um, hi," Morrison said timidly into the microphone. A little bit of feedback squelched through the gymnasium speakers.

"Hey man, let's play!" shouted the Phlegm bass player.

"Um, right," said Jim, nervously fingering the guitar that the lead singer had loaned to him. He tentatively strummed the instrument. Wrong chord. More feedback.

"What's going on?" Taps cried, rushing over to Trevor and Chip. "He looks terrible up there."

"Ten bucks says he recycles his lunch," Trevor replied, not taking his eyes off the stage, where Morrison was not doing very well. He was so pale that the spotlight was practically shining right through him and Phlegm was getting impatient.

"Hey dude, what are you waiting for?" hissed the lead singer. "This ain't karaoke, you know."

Morrison would have been doomed, except when he squinted into the lights, he managed to make out a familiar face in the audience. Right in the front row was the pretty face of Caitlin Burrack. Morrison snapped back to reality.

"Okay, this is a song I wrote for a special girl who doesn't think I'm special at all," Morrison paused and stared right at Caitlin. "I just wrote it today. Sorry it doesn't totally rhyme."

Gripping the guitar with authority, Morrison ripped into a gritty grunge-rock riff. The members of Phlegm crashed in behind him, going full speed and barely keeping up with the possessed Morrison who was now howling into the microphone:

She's got a funky nose ring in her nose,
She wears these funky skateboarding clothes,
She can curse me out just like a truck driver,
She looks like that girl who's on MTV!
(Drum break)
She's Caitlin! Caitlin! Caitlin!

She's way too cool for me!
She's Caitlin! Caitlin! Caitlin!
I bet she's got tattoos where you can't see!

Morrison, momentarily forgetting the next lyric, launched into a spontaneous guitar solo, hurling a barrage of rock rhythms into the crowd from his six-string assault weapon. Near the middle of the gym, an astonished Trevor leaned over to yell into Chip's ear.

"Is he doing what I think he's doing?"

"Making a complete dork of himself?"

"Yes."

"Yes, indeed he is!"

"Do you think we should —"

"Wait!" Chip held up his hand. "Here comes the second verse!"

She's got purple streaks in her hair!
People point and stare but she don't care!
She probably hates me 'cause I shop at The Bay!
It's not my fault, my mom makes me go there!
She's Caitlin! Caitlin! Caitlin!
She's way too cool for me!
She's Caitlin! Caitlin! Caitlin!
I'll pierce my nose if you'll go out with me!

As the other members of Phlegm thrashed wildly on stage, Morrison tossed his guitar to one side and took a stage dive into the crowd.

"Oh no," cried Taps. "They're going to kill him!" Even Chip was knocked speechless as Morrison crowd-surfed on the first ten rows of students before being thrown back onto the stage. Morrison whipped off a few more crazy riffs on his guitar before high-fiving the bass player.

"Okay, here's the plan," cried Chip, suddenly all business. "Taps, you create a diversion. Big and I will get Morrison out of here before they can pound him to a pulp. Let's move."

"Hey, what do I do?" Trevor piped in.

"Either run or pray," Chip shot back. "This could be ugly."

Still rocking, Morrison was now throwing himself around onstage in a wild frenzy. He was writhing on the floor and playing his guitar like a man possessed. In fact, he had already broken two strings on the guitar, but showed no signs of slowing down.

"Okay, here's the last verse," Morrison hollered. But, he would never get to the last verse. After all his thrashing about on stage, Morrison's feet had become thoroughly tangled up in the guitar cord. Taking two steps toward the centre of the stage, Morrison tripped and fell flat on the guitar.

A shriek of feedback echoed through the gym before Morrison moved his legs once more, mercifully ripping the guitar cord out of the amplifier and leaving the gym quiet.

The rest of the band gradually stopped playing as they noticed Morrison struggling to get back on his feet. With his feet hog-tied, Morrison awkwardly righted himself and stared out into the silent gymnasium.

From the back, someone let out a loud cough.

"Thank you, QEH!" Morrison shouted, giving a little wave, and wobbling on his feet. "Good night!"

There was another moment of awkward silence.

"Let's get him, guys," Chip said as the Grizzly Bears raced to the front of the gymnasium to save their teammate from what seemed like certain doom.

Before they reached the stage, another sound filled the gymnasium. Applause. It started with three spaced-out, long-haired rockers in the front clapping slowly, but it quickly spread until all four hundred kids in the gymnasium were wildly cheering, clapping, and screaming.

"That was the most kickin' set we've ever had, man," the lead singer of Phlegm screamed at a shocked Jim Morrison. "You definitely do not suck!"

The other members of the band crowded around the stunned Morrison, slapping him on the back and offering their congratulations.

"Yeah man, you rock," chimed in the Phlegm drummer. "Can we do that song at our next gig?"

"Yeah. Yeah, sure," Morrison blinked several times, looking like a man coming out of a trance. "Go ahead. It's yours."

"Morrison, hang on, pal," yelled Big reaching the bottom of the stairs. "We're coming, buddy."

"Oh no," cried Trevor, "one of them's got him in a headlock."

Up on the stage, Morrison was being wrapped up by a small figure. Poking his head out, Morrison spotted his friends at the foot of the stage and started to wave his hands.

"Look! He can't breathe!" Chip cried, racing onto the stage to help his friend. "Big, get that guy off of him!"

"Um, Chip," Big said. "I don't think Morrison wants that guy off of him."

Chip didn't get it. "Why do you say that?"

"Because that guy's a girl," Big said pointing.

Sure enough, Jim Morrison and Caitlin Burrack were in the middle of the stage, wrapped up in each others' arms.

Chip was momentarily stunned. "What a guy," he mumbled, turning around and walking down the stage steps. "How does he do it?"

The QEH dance was over shortly after Morrison's impromptu performance. Even before all of the students had drifted out of the gymnasium, janitors were wiping down the floor, setting up chairs, and making the place ready for the basketball games which would resume the next morning.

"Where have you losers been?"

The Bears wheeled around to see Langdon Strong

racing toward them. "You guys are one hour late for curfew," he sneered with a cruel smile. "And you, Carson — Coach Kenny *really* wants to see you."

Chip shot Langdon a nasty look but said nothing. As much as Chip hated it, Langdon was right — they were late for curfew.

"He's right," Trevor whispered, glancing at his wrist watch.

"I know he's right," Chip hissed, turning to Morrison, still locked in Caitlin's arms. "Hey, Romeo! We're late for curfew, let's go."

The Bears were halfway to the door when Chip remembered he had left his red duffel bag beside the refreshment table.

"I'll be right back," he called racing over to where he had stowed his bag. "Hey, it's gone!" he shouted. "Anyone seen my stuff?"

"The janitor probably picked it up," yelled Trevor. "Come on, you can get it later."

Chip had one more look around before trotting after his teammates.

The boys had barely left the gym when they ran headlong into Coach Kenny and a very serious looking woman in a blue skirt and blazer. Chip was relieved to see Coach Kenny carrying his red duffel bag. He wouldn't be relieved for very long, however.

"Coach Kenny," Chip said, panting and throwing his arms around his coach. "We are so glad to see you.

So sorry we're late, but we were just minding our own business at the dance when we learned that there was a forest fire in the next county. Well, we just couldn't stand the idea of those little trees getting roasted, so we volunteered to help fight the fire! But when we got there it was much worse than we imagined and poor Big tried to rescue a family of squirrels and got overcome by smoke and we had to take him to the hospital, right Big?"

Big shot Chip a strange look. "Yeah, right," the big boy coughed awkwardly.

"And then, on the way back —"

"Can it, Carson," Coach Kenny said sharply, sounding genuinely angry with his players. "Guys, this is Principal Hillard. She'd like to talk to you for a minute."

Principal Hillard was tall and slim and not amused. She was an attractive middle-aged woman who looked as if she hadn't smiled for some time.

"Boys, something serious happened tonight at the dance," she began gravely. "Someone put alcohol in our punch bowls."

The Bears exchanged puzzled looks. They expected to catch heck for being late, but this caught them off guard. How did this pertain to them?

"Do you know who did it?" Chip asked innocently.

"We have an idea," Coach Kenny shot back. "Is this your bag, Carson?"

"Yeah, it is," he nodded.

"Well, this is what we found in it," Coach Kenny said, pulling a half-empty bottle of booze from the folds of Chip's duffel bag.

Even though he knew he didn't do anything wrong, Chip felt himself getting red in the face. "I didn't do it," he protested. For once, Chip knew this wasn't a time for a smart comment.

"I don't know what things are like at your school," Principal Hillard, said sternly. "But we have a very strict alcohol policy at QEH. Any student caught with it is suspended immediately."

"But I wasn't caught with it," Chip finally managed to speak. "You found it in my gym bag."

"And how do you explain that?" Principal Hillard replied.

"Who knows?" Chip cried. "Maybe someone put it there when I wasn't looking!"

Principal Hillard didn't have the time to play detective. "I have no doubt that you or one of your teammates put alcohol in our punch," she said decisively. "If you did it, I have no choice other than to suspend you from playing tomorrow. If you refuse to admit your guilt, then I will have no choice but to disqualify your team." Principal Hillard glared at Coach Kenny. "Can I leave it you to sort this matter out?"

Coach Kenny nodded as Principal Hillard spun on her heels and stalked down the hallway.

"Well?" Coach Kenny said. Obviously he wasn't

going to give Chip the benefit of the doubt for this prank.

Chip looked beseechingly at his teammates for help. All of them were staring intently at the floor except for Langdon, who was smirking at Chip.

He was trapped. Chip knew that if his team was disqualified, Coach Kenny would be fired for sure. But if he took the heat, there was still a chance that they would win tomorrow. Chip was certain Langdon had planted the bottle in his bag, but right now there was no way to prove it. Chip gnawed at his bottom lip.

"Okay," he said finally. "I guess I did it."

8 BIOLOGY 101

Big McMann should have been one happy guy. He was on a road trip with all his friends from school and his team was headed into the finals of the biggest basketball tournament in the province. Despite all that, after the last night's events he was pretty bummed out.

Without Chip starting at guard, the Bears had little chance of even holding their own in the finals, let alone actually winning the game. On top of that, the Monday deadline for his biology assignment was looming and at this point, the project was no closer to being finished than it had been when he had left Cape Breton.

Big plodded down the long hall toward the library with all the enthusiasm of a man headed to a broccoli-eating contest. He had decided to make one more attempt at finishing his project. He only hoped Stanley was finished with the textbook.

As he reached the double glass doors of the library, Big took a deep breath and tried to formulate a plan. Nothing happened. Shaking his head, Big once again walked into the QEH library.

Behind the desk, the perky librarian greeted Big with a grin. "Back to finish your homework, huh?" he asked cheerfully.

"Um, yeah," Big said quietly. "Is ... *he* ... still here?"

The grey-haired man smiled benignly. "I'm afraid so, but go ask him. He may be done with that textbook now. I'm sorry we don't have another copy for you."

Big shrugged. "No problem."

Looking across the library, Big could see the top of Stanley's head as the boy was immersed in his reading. Coming closer, Big was dismayed to see that Stanley was still reading from the same textbook Big needed. The Grizzly Bear centre padded quietly toward Stanley.

"Ahem," Big coughed.

"Oh good, you're back," Stanley said with mock sincerity. "I was actually getting some studying done."

"Sorry to bother you again," Big replied. "But are you any closer to being finished with that book?" Big never looked for a confrontation under normal circumstances and he certainly wasn't to going to pick a fight with Stanley, no matter how rude the boy was.

"A little," Stanley said. "But don't hold your breath. I'm swamped."

Big looked at the stacks of other books, and bit his lip. "Um, I just have to make some notes from one chapter in that textbook. I've looked everywhere else, it's not online, and I can't find the same information anywhere. Isn't there something in these other books that you can study for just a little while?"

Stanley tensed up and shoved the book across the table at Big. "You want the book? Fine. Take it," Stanley snapped. "I'm going down in flames here and I'm none too happy about it. This test is going to kill me. I mean, I know nothing and if I bomb this test it's going to kill my average. If it kills my average, I may fail the year." Stanley paused and glared angrily at Big. "So here's your book. Take your time. I could read that textbook for a hundred hours and I'll never know it any better." Stanley pushed the book closer to Big. "Go ahead, take it," he instructed.

Big stared down at the page where Stanley had left the book open. He instantly recognized the material.

"Is this the stuff you're doing?" Big asked, cautiously bending over and picking up the textbook.

Stanley nodded miserably.

"This is photosynthesis," Big said, flipping a few pages and scanning the diagrams. "It's how plants make food from sunlight. I studied this last term." Big looked at Stanley. "You know, if you want, I can help you with this."

Stanley was caught off guard. It was obvious no one had ever offered to help him with anything before. "You'd do that?" he asked uncertainly.

"Sure," Big replied. "Do you mind if I sit down?"

"If you want to." Stanley sounded as if he definitely

wanted Big to help. "I mean, after I was such a jerk to you and your friend."

Big shrugged, and folded himself into the orange plastic chair beside Stanley. "You were stressed," he replied. "Everyone acts weird when they're stressed. When I'm stressed, I clean my room. Sometimes, during exams, my room gets so clean I have to throw stuff on the floor just so I can straighten it up again."

Stanley laughed. "I am so freaked out over this. My dad will kill me if they hold me back a grade."

"Relax," Big said, reassuringly. "I personally guarantee that after I show you a couple of tricks, you'll be more than ready to pass that test tomorrow."

When it came to biology, Big definitely knew his stuff. As the friendly giant went over the various sketches, diagrams, and definitions, it was clear that Stanley was getting it. Big even supplied him with some memory tricks to help him with the more complicated explanations.

The two boys talked biology for almost twenty minutes and Stanley was catching on fast. He was actually a pleasant guy when he wasn't strung as taut as a high wire. In fact, once the two started talking, it turned out that Stanley's family had a cottage in the same part of Cape Breton where Big lived. Stanley had spent several of his summers at a camp where Big's older brother worked as a counsellor.

"You know," Stanley said. "When I first saw you

and your buddy in the library, I thought you were a couple of basketball boneheads coming to stuff me in a garbage can."

Big let out a little laugh. "Why did you think that?"

Stanley smiled. "Because jocks always do that to me. They like to pick on me because I'm small and a little shy. Sometimes I just don't know quite how to act."

"Act like yourself," Big said finally. "If people don't like it, then at least you've given them a shot to know who you are." The two guys sat in silence for a moment before Big got up off the chair. "Anyway, it was nice to meet you. I'll see you around, I guess. Good luck on the test."

Big started walking out the door of the library when Stanley called out to him.

"Hey Matt," he yelled. Big turned around and saw that Stanley was holding up the textbook for him. "I'm finished with this now," Stanley said. "Just put it back on the shelf when you're done."

Big smiled as he took the book from Stanley. "Thanks," Big said sincerely.

★ ★ ★

Chip Carson had had better days.

Lying on the bed in his drab hotel room, Chip reflected on the muddle of events that had occurred last evening.

It was clear that Langdon had set him up. He knew it and everyone else on the team knew it too. What really bugged him was that Coach Kenny was so quick to lose faith in him — especially when all Chip wanted to do was make sure Coach Kenny didn't get fired. One thing was for certain, when word got back that the Grizzly Bears were fooling around with booze, Coach Kenny would be fired for sure.

Chip sighed heavily and tossed a pillow across the room in frustration. Two weeks ago, Chip's mind would be busy coming up with a scheme to get back at Langdon, but right now he could care less about evening the score. Chip was more concerned that in a few hours his Bears would be getting smoked by the Cartier Academy Wildcats and he would be forced to sit on the bench and watch the slaughter. It seemed like as soon as he had started to really care about the team, the whole thing had fallen apart.

Chip looked out the window and stared at the low-lying QEH school building directly across the street. He glanced at his watch. He still had six hours to figure a way out of the mess. No problem.

★ ★ ★

The QEH cafeteria was practically empty on the second day of the tournament. Several teams had been knocked out of contention and had left the previous night. By the end of the day, one remaining team would be named champion.

At a table near the back of the cafeteria, Trevor, Taps, Morrison, Langdon, and a few of the other Bears were silently munching their pre-game lunch. For a team heading into the finals, no one was in a very good mood, with the exception of Langdon.

The Bears' superstar had a lot of nerve sitting down with his teammates. Nonetheless, Langdon was positively glowing as he started to eat his lunch.

"So, Trevor," Langdon said with a large, plastic grin, "I guess you're going to be giving me all those assists today, since Chip won't be able to play?"

Trevor barely lifted his eyes from his plate. "Go gargle sand, Langdon," he growled.

"My, aren't we in a bad mood?" Langdon sang out cheerily. "How about you, Jim?" he continued, totally undaunted. "Maybe you can borrow Chip's sneakers, since I don't think he'll be needing them."

"Shut up, Langdon," Morrison shot back. "Everyone knows it was you who pulled that dirty stunt on Chip last night."

"I did no such thing," Langdon said, looking hurt. "Just because our little misguided friend Chip is becoming a booze-hound at such a young age, I don't think you should try to blame it on me. After all, I think Coach Kenny and the QEH principal know best. If they don't think Chip should play, as an upstanding young person, I have no choice but to support their decision."

"Would you just leave us alone, Langdon?" Taps cried from the far side of the table. "I don't think anyone really wants to listen to you right now."

"Shut up, Taps," Langdon shot back. "I don't have to take any crap from a water boy like you. I'll sit anywhere I want."

Langdon was still mouthing off to his teammates when Big McMann returned from the library. In Big's hands was a stack of papers that he carried as if they were gold. Big had finished his biology project and he was very happy. Until he saw Langdon at the table.

"What are you doing here?" Big yelled, losing his temper and slamming down the stack of papers on the table top with a thunderous bang.

Langdon looked way up at the glaring Big and lost his cocksure attitude in a hurry. "I was just leaving," he said meekly, stumbling away from the table and beating a hasty retreat.

Big and the rest of the Bears just glared as their unpopular scoring leader walked briskly out of the cafeteria, without so much as a backward glance. To make sure Langdon had truly departed, Big followed him out of the cafeteria and watched him disappear down the hall.

"Bunch of losers," Langdon grumbled as he stalked through the hallways of Queen Elizabeth High looking for a place to hang out until game time.

The Bears superstar turned down a long hallway beside the gymnasium and heard voices coming from an open classroom. Curious, Langdon poked his head in and saw several members of the Cartier Academy Wildcats getting ready for their final game against Langdon's Bears.

"Hey, it's one of the ferocious Grizzly Bears," laughed one of the Cartier Academy players, noticing Langdon at the door. "Grrrrr!"

"Oh, sorry guys," Langdon said, withdrawing his head and starting to walk away.

"That's okay," another Wildcat shouted. "Come on in!"

Langdon tentatively entered the makeshift dressing room. On a row of hooks near the door, the Wildcats' purple uniforms were hung neatly. Because it was still too early to start getting changed, the Cartier Academy players lounged around the room in their street clothes. Some had their headphones on, others were playing portable video games, and a few others were engaged in a game of cards in the corner.

"Hey, you're number twelve, right?" piped up Chad, the wiry Wildcat who had had the run-in with Chip and Big in Super Burger the other day.

"Yeah," Langdon said coolly, liking the fact that the opposing team had noticed him on the court.

"Where's the rest of your team?" asked a guy in

the corner who had a sharp buzzcut with two purple streaks dyed along the sides.

"Cafeteria," Langdon replied without much interest.

"You not hungry?"

"I had other things to do."

"I was watching you during your last game," Chad said from his perch on top of the front desk. "You think you're hot stuff, don't you?"

"I don't know," Langdon said smugly. "I average seventeen points and nine rebounds per game. What do you think?"

"You can get as many points as you want," piped up the guy with the purple streaks. "The rest of your team is a complete joke."

"Yeah, well, so is your haircut," Langdon shot back. The Wildcats were shocked for a moment before grinning amongst themselves. A couple of the bigger players started to move menacingly toward Langdon.

Langdon Strong would never win any team spirit awards, but he wasn't going to let the guys from Cartier Academy talk badly about his team, even though he was standing in the middle of their dressing room.

If he knew how nasty the Wildcats could be, he would have kept his mouth shut.

9 A CLOSE SHAVE

"This stinks," Trevor grumbled as he walked down the hallway toward the classroom that served as the Bears' dressing room. Big and a few of his teammates nodded their agreement.

It was three hours before game time and Coach Kenny had called a team meeting. After all that had happened, team spirit was pretty dismal.

"Hey Chip," Taps began nervously. "Are you sure Coach Kenny won't be mad at you for coming to this meeting, after, you know, last night?"

Chip shrugged his shoulders. "I was suspended from the game, Taps, not meetings. After all, I'm still part of this team, right?"

Taps nodded quickly.

When the Bears reached their dressing room, they found the door open a crack. This was a little strange, because only Coach Kenny had a key and he was never early for a team meeting. As the guys cautiously pushed the door open, their jaws dropped.

Someone had trashed their dressing room. Wet toilet paper had been strewn around the room and toothpaste had been squirted all over the boys' uniforms. Old bananas had been squished into their sneakers and dirty words had been scrawled all over the chalkboard along with the message, "You losers won't be so lucky this time." It was signed, "With love, The Wildcats."

Totally unnerved, the guys could only stand and stare at the mess in front of them.

"Those creeps," Trevor said finally. "I hate those jerks from Cartier Academy."

"Yeah," Big said quietly, sitting down heavily on the only clean chair in the room.

The boys sat in stunned silence for several minutes until Coach Kenny burst into the room. He took one look at the mess and then the silence was over.

"Oh man!" he cried, not believing the mess that he was seeing. "What happened here? Who did this?"

No one answered the coach and that just made him more angry.

"Look, if you don't tell me who made this mess, we're going to have to forfeit our game," Coach Kenny said gravely. "I know you guys are upset that Chip is suspended, but you can't just vandalize school property. I thought you guys knew better than that."

"We didn't do it, Coach," Trevor said. "The Cartier Academy Wildcats did!"

"How do you know that?" Coach Kenny frowned.

Trevor pointed at the blackboard where the nasty messages had yet to be erased. "They signed their name!"

Coach Kenny shook his head and stayed angry, although it was clear he was now angry at the Wildcats. "When I call a team meeting at three o'clock, you guys be here at three o'clock!" Coach Kenny glared at his team. "We've got warm-ups in twenty minutes. Get your uniforms on. I want you out on the court in ten minutes." The coach stomped toward the door. "I've got to go take care of Cartier Academy. I'll be in the principal's office if anyone needs me. Get changed." For the first time, Kenny sounded as if he had the confidence of a real coach.

The Bears sat around the room for a few minutes in total silence. A few heads popped up as the guys heard a girl's laughter coming from outside the door and Morrison and Caitlin walked into the room holding hands.

"Oh my," Caitlin said, stopping short at the sight of the room.

"What happened?" Morrison asked.

"Wildcats," mumbled Taps, weakly gesturing to the blackboard.

Morrison said nothing. The sombre mood was contagious and Morrison and Caitlin leaned up against the wall and stared at the mess. As the rest of the team trickled into the room, they quickly joined their crestfallen teammates in silence, no one saying a word, no one making a move to clean up. The Bears were a beaten bunch.

The clincher came as Langdon Strong walked into the room. His eyes were red and looked as if he had been crying. That really didn't matter, because no one was looking at Langdon's face. Everyone was staring at his head. The Wildcats had shaved Langdon bald!

"What happened to you?" cried a shocked Big.

"Wildcats," mumbled Langdon, his gaze focused on the floor.

"All right," cried Chip, hopping to his feet and turning to his teammates. "That's it! I don't know about you guys, but I've had enough."

"Shut up, Carson," snapped Langdon through clenched teeth. "As if you care."

"About you? Not really," Chip confessed. "I do care about this team, though. A lot. We're a good bunch of guys and I'm sick of us being treated like chumps! Look at us. We're headed into the provincial finals and because someone trashes our change room we're suddenly moping around like the losers everyone else says we are."

"What do you think we should do, Chip?" Trevor asked expectantly.

"Two words, baby," Chip declared loudly. "Re-venge!"

"That's only one word, Chip," Taps pointed out from the back of the room.

"Not the way I do it!"

"What are we going to do?" Trevor asked.

Chip bit his lip. "I don't have a clue, but you can start by getting us some toothpaste, super glue, and anything rotting in the cafeteria — which, judging from lunch, could be just about everything — and a case of toilet paper."

"Wait a second," Caitlin interrupted. "Are you planning to trash their dressing room?"

Chip looked at the girl blankly. "That was the general direction of my plan. Why?"

"Oh, no reason," Caitlin said pointedly. "It's just such a brilliant display of maturity, that's all. I'm very impressed by your knee-jerk, super-macho reaction to the situation."

Chip turned to Morrison. "I get the feeling she's being a little sarcastic," he whispered loudly.

Morrison shrugged.

"Look, Caitlin," Chip continued. "In case you didn't notice, the Wildcats have trashed our room. What are we supposed to do, send them a thank you note? I think we need to show them that they can't do that to us. We definitely need to get them back."

"By sinking to their level?" Caitlin replied.

Chip rolled his eyes. "I'm sorry. And you think we should deal with this . . . how?"

"I don't know. They probably trashed the room to psych you guys out."

"And?"

"And if you start running around worrying about how to even the score, then I guess it will have worked. You guys are so psyched out, you're not even thinking about the game you have to play. You're not thinking about how far you've come as a team. You're not thinking about how good your chances are of winning this tournament. They've totally thrown you off your game."

Caitlin paused to let her words sink in.

"You've got to show them that little stunts like this don't bother you. Show them you're above their immature pranks. Yes, Chip, I do know a better way you can get even with these guys."

Chip raised his eyebrows in anticipation. "And how's that?"

"Get out on the court and kick their butts."

Chip looked at Caitlin and bit his lip. "Are you guys cool with that?" He said turning and staring hard at his teammates. A few guys nodded their heads in agreement. "All right, then," Chip cried, bending down and straightening a desk that had knocked over. "Let's settle this out on the court. Let's show 'em just what the Cape Breton Grizzly Bears can do when we're ticked off. Nobody messes with us. Let's go rip these clowns apart. What do you guys say?"

The Grizzly Bears cheered loudly and high-fived each other. The team was no longer blindly angry at the Wildcats and each boy had a steely look of determination in his eye. The Grizzly Bears were ready to play.

The only person who was still unsatisfied was Langdon.

"Come on, Langdon," Big shouted, tugging his

uniform jersey over his massive shoulders. "Let's have a good game out there."

Langdon mumbled a lukewarm response. He was preoccupied with his hair, or lack of it. "I look like a total freak," he said finally.

"You're right," replied Chip, who was changing into his uniform despite the fact that he was benched for the finals. "You do look like a freak. We should do something about that."

Langdon cocked his head and waited for Chip's wisecrack. None came. Instead, Chip walked over and fished around in Big's giant duffel bag.

"Ah, here it is," Chip said finally, producing the electric razor that Big used to keep his brush cut tidy.

"What are you doing?" cried Langdon, covering his head with his hands. "There's nothing left for you to cut!"

"Shave it down to the wood, Big," Chip instructed, taking a seat and handing the big boy the clippers.

"You want me to cut your hair?" Big asked, raising his eyebrows.

"No I don't want you to cut it," Chip replied shortly. "I want you shave it. Bald — just like Langdon."

"Are you sure?" Big said, flipping on the electric razor.

"Yeah, I'm sure." Chip said. "You're going to shave everyone bald. Then I'm going to shave you."

Big smiled, catching onto Chip's scheme. "All righty

then," the big boy called, swiping the razor down the middle of Chip's head. Within a minute Chip's head was as smooth as a billiard ball.

"Next!" cried Chip, grabbing the clippers and facing his teammates. No one moved. "Aw, c'mon guys," Chip shouted "Who's next?"

"Um, Chip, isn't this a bit drastic?" Morrison said quietly.

"Absolutely not," yelled Chip. "When those guys shaved Langdon's head, they wanted him to look stupid. Well, he can't look stupid if everyone on the team looks the same."

"I don't care if he looks stupid, he's a jerk," a voice called out near the back of the room. A murmur of agreement went up from the rest of guys.

"Hey, listen up!" Chip yelled, hopping on a chair and waving his arms like a man possessed. "Langdon's our teammate. No matter what you think of him personally, he's part of our team. When those guys shaved Langdon's head, they disrespected every one of us. They tried to show us up. Well, they can't mess with us. They can't touch us. We are about to win the provincial championship! But we can't do that unless we are twelve guys playing together as a team. Now let's show some team spirit. Let's show some unity. Let's show these clowns that they can't mess with the Bears!"

Chip paused to let his words sink in. No one said anything. Finally Trevor stepped forward.

"You know," he said, slowly running his fingers through his dark hair. "Now that you mention it, I am due for a trim."

Chip smiled as his friend sat down in the chair. "We're going to kick some butt out there," Chip said, squaring his shoulders.

With a few quick strokes Trevor was buzzed bald. When Trevor was finished, there was another brief pause before Morrison agreed to show some scalp. The rest of the team quickly fell in line and within ten minutes the floor was covered with hair, and Chip was surrounded by bald teammates.

Each buzzcut was met with cheers, high-fives, and much head rubbing. By the time the timid Taps took the chair, the bald Grizzly Bears were psyched up to frenzy level.

"My mom is going to kill me," Taps mumbled, grimacing as Chip shaved his head.

"Tell her she's going to save a fortune on shampoo," laughed Trevor, giving his teammate a gentle head butt. The entire team erupted into wild cheering as the last Bear was rendered hairless.

Chip once again popped up on a nearby chair.

"You guys look beautiful!" he screamed amidst the laughter and cheers. "Now get out there and make these punks look ugly!"

Cheers and thunderous applause filled the tiny classroom as twelve boisterous, bald teenagers bolted out the door. Ready to play the biggest game of their lives, the team was so hyped they would have run through a brick wall if Chip had told them to. The Cartier Academy Wildcats actually seemed beatable.

Langdon Strong was the last Bear out the door.

"Um, thanks, Chip," he said quietly.

"Don't thank me," Chip replied crisply. "I didn't do it for you. I did it for the team."

"Well, you didn't have to do it at all, so thanks," Langdon said finally.

Chip shrugged.

"And Chip," Langdon continued. "I guess I'm sorry for what happened last night, but I didn't have anything to do with it."

"Whatever," Chip shrugged again. "Langdon, you always talk about scoring a lot of points. You know, this game we really need you to do it."

Langdon shook Chip's hand and stared him straight in the eye.

"Done," he said firmly.

10 NOTHING BUT NET

As the Grizzly Bears gathered outside the gymnasium, waiting to take the floor for their warm-ups, the energy was tangible. The boys' hearts were pounding as fast as the thumping rhythms of the techno music blasting in the gym, and there was an air of determination about the team. They were going in as the underdogs and they knew it, but they had resolved not to lose. Forming a single line and jogging into the gym, the Grizzly Bears took the court.

Coach Kenny, meanwhile, was facing the biggest game he had ever coached and his antiperspirant was no match for the nervous sweat running from every pore of his body. Everyone knew this was Coach Kenny's one shot at glory. No Cape Breton coach had ever come home with the provincial title. In fact, Coach Kenny was so careless that people would be surprised if he came home without losing any players.

On the end of the bench, Chip Carson was burning to get up and start shooting some hoops. He clenched his teeth. For this game, he may as well have his shorts stapled to the pine.

"Let's go, guys!" he cried, clapping his hands. Despite the fact that he was benched, Chip was determined to do anything he could to help his team win.

The game buzzer sounded, signalling the end of warm-ups, and the Grizzly Bears crowded around Coach Kenny for their last minute instructions.

"Okay guys, this is it," the young man yelled over the pounding music and buzz of the crowd. "So let's get out there and play smart. I want to see good shots and tough defence." Coach Kenny sounded confident and even believable as he barked out the last-minute instructions. "I know we can win this," he bellowed. "Now get out there and do it."

The Grizzly Bears broke from the huddle with a booming cheer, each starter making a point to slap five with Chip before taking the floor. Chip stayed on his feet long after everyone else had taken a seat on the bench, watching intently as Big narrowly lost the opening jump ball and the Grizzly Bears retreated to play defence on the first play of the game.

Coming down the court, the wiry point guard, Chad, dribbled patiently at the top of the key as the Cartier Academy big men went to work. As the centre battled with Big for position under the hoop, the Wildcat power forward popped out to set a screen for Chad.

"Roll, roll!" yelled Chad as he used the pick, then

dropped a perfect bounce pass as the forward rolled to the hoop for a little drop-in.

Over on the bench, Taps leaned over and whispered to an antsy Chip. "You know, if we win, it will be the first time ever the championship has been won by a team with zero regular season wins."

Chip chewed nervously on a towel. "Great stat, Taps."

On the attack, Trevor raced downcourt only to run headlong into a Wildcat defensive trap. Double-teamed, Trevor frantically searched for someone to pass to. Finally, he flipped the ball over to Langdon who was hovering around mid-court.

Langdon wasted no time in shaking his defender with a nifty between-the-legs dribble. The tall forward then spotted up at the three-point line before letting fly a pretty rainbow jumper.

"Yes!" Chip caught himself cheering as Langdon's three-pointer found the bottom of the bucket. The Bears were up, three to two.

Cartier Academy inbounded the ball with a lazy pass to their guard. Trevor neatly stole the lobbed ball away from the opposing player and fired it to Langdon, who was still parked under the hoop. The Bears' bench erupted as Langdon scored again.

As the Wildcats brought the ball down the court, Chip noticed that their opponents were going with a three-guard offence. That would allow Cartier Academy a faster, better shooting team on the floor, but it also could cause problems defensively.

"There's got to be a mismatch, down low," Chip said softly, running over and talking into his coach's ear. "Give the ball to Big in the post!"

Coach Kenny was unsure what Chip meant, but had the sense to trust his starting guard.

"There's a mismatch down low!" Coach Kenny shouted as Cartier Academy made another basket. "Get the ball to Big!"

Trevor nodded and waved for his teammates to clear out one side of the court to give Big room to operate. Catching Trevor's shovel pass, Big bulldozed his way over the smaller Cartier Academy player who was trying to guard him and banked in the shot.

Coach Kenny glanced over at Chip.

"Good call, Coach," Chip cried loudly.

Through the first eight minutes of the game, the Grizzly Bears managed to hang fairly close to Cartier Academy. That was largely thanks to a red-hot-shooting Langdon Strong.

The Bears forward had made four of five shots and was three for three at the line. He was also exhausted.

"Sub!" Langdon cried the next time he passed the bench.

Coach Kenny bit his lip. "Morrison," he winced. "Get in there."

"My pleasure, Coach!" Morrison shouted, springing off the bench and trotting to the scorers' table, stopping only to show off his brand new basketball sneakers to Coach Kenny. "Cool, huh?" he grinned. "Caitlin took me shopping."

Coach Kenny tried not to smile.

With Langdon out of the game, Cartier Academy quickly opened up a lead. The Bears just didn't have the depth to keep up with the waves of Wildcats coming off the bench. With each trip down the court, the Cape Breton team saw their hopes of a championship slip farther away from them.

"Set it up," called Chad, running the floor and waiting for his teammates to find their places. The Cartier Academy half-court offence was firing with precision accuracy. With each player either setting a pick or cutting to the hoop, the Wildcats were having no trouble finding easy shots. It didn't help matters when Big collected his third foul with five minutes left in the half and had to go to the bench.

By the time the horn sounded to end the first sixteen minutes of play, the Grizzly Bears were down by twelve. With their floor general benched, their hopes of getting back in the game were dim.

The Grizzly Bears' locker room at halftime wasn't pretty. Coach Kenny did his best to get his team fired up, but he was simply overwhelmed by the circumstances.

"Come on, guys," he said with all the enthusiasm he could muster. "This is our last game of the year. Let's do all we can to win!"

"We *are* doing all we can to win," grumbled Trevor. "They're doing all they can do too. And they're better than us."

Coach Kenny pretended not to hear and called out several set plays that he wanted to try in the second half.

"Let's start the second half with a full-court press," he called as he sent his team back out on the floor.

As the Grizzly Bears were finishing up their half-time shoot-around, Morrison noticed Caitlin waving at him from her seat in the bleachers.

"Hey Caitlin," Morrison said glumly, trudging over to his new girlfriend.

"Hey Jim, nice try out there," she said. It really wasn't like her to come to sporting events — especially ones that involved school.

"Yeah, well, you know," Morrison mumbled.

"How come Chip isn't playing?" Caitlin asked. "I thought you said he was one of your best players?"

"He is," Morrison said. "But Coach Kenny benched him because he thinks Chip spiked the punch at the dance last night."

"He didn't," Caitlin replied.

"I know, Langdon did and pinned the whole thing on Chip and now we don't have a point guard and we're going to lose the game."

"Langdon didn't spike the punch either," Caitlin said quickly.

Morrison gave her a puzzled look. "How do you know that?"

"Because I did," she said, twiddling her nose ring.

"What?" Morrison couldn't believe what he was hearing.

Caitlin shrugged. "How could anyone else do it, anyway?" she asked. "I was stuck at that stupid punch table all night. Of course I did it."

"Will you tell that to my coach?" Morrison had to ask.

"Sure," Caitlin said nonchalantly.

"You know he'll have to tell your principal," Morrison said, hesitating to get Caitlin in trouble.

"Oh yeah, she'll probably yell at me, then maybe kick me out of school for a few days. Big deal," Caitlin said. "She doesn't scare me."

Morrison didn't agree. "Are you sure? She seemed pretty harsh to me."

Caitlin let out a little laugh. "She's my mom, you dork."

Morrison didn't have time to be confused. The horn sounded, starting the second half, and Caitlin was already trotting across the gym floor, nearly knocking down a referee who happened to be in her way. Morrison watched as Caitlin whispered something in Coach Kenny's ear.

The young man's eyes lit up like a Christmas tree.

"Are you serious?" he asked, not believing what he was hearing.

Caitlin nodded.

"Carson!" Coach Kenny bellowed. "Get in there!"

"Um, I'm benched, Coach." Chip raised his eyebrows. "Remember?"

"Well, I'm your coach and I'm un-benching you. Now get in there!"

Puzzled, but more than ready to play, Chip raced to the scorers' table and checked into the game.

"What are you doing?" asked Trevor, shocked to see his teammate out of the floor.

"Playing, apparently," Chip said simply. "Now let's kick these losers off our court."

Trevor cracked a crooked smile and nodded slowly.

"Hey, nice to see you, Cha," Chip said amicably, sizing up his opponent and turning around so his back faced the Wildcat point guard. "Get used to this view, pal, 'cause you're going to be seeing it a lot as I go by you."

The Wildcat point guard stared daggers at Chip. "My name's Chad," was all he said.

With Chip in the backcourt handling the ball, the Grizzly Bears got off to a great start. Every pass was razor-sharp and everyone was in sync on the floor. Especially after sitting out the entire first half, Chip was fully energized and running circles around any Wildcat who tried to stop him.

In the first six minutes, the Bears had gnawed into the Wildcat lead and were only down by eight.

"Let's go, guys!" shouted Chip, catching a long

Wildcat rebound and streaking down the court. "Let's push it. Let's run these losers into the ground."

Chip took one step over the half-court line and was met by Chad frantically trying to get into defensive position. Chip was having none of it, spinning off of the Academy guard and cutting to the centre of the floor.

Taking a quick glance behind him, Chip saw that Big was running close behind. The slick Cape Breton guard accelerated to the hoop, looking as if he was going to go all the way. When two huge Wildcats stepped in to help, Chip dropped a no-look pass between his legs to the trailing Big, who scored the layup.

Back on defence, the Wildcats were struggling to get anything going. The Grizzly Bears had really stepped it up in the middle and were challenging every shot the Wildcats took. Big had more blocks than a box of Lego and even Morrison had come over to make a couple of rejections.

"This is my house!" hollered Big, sending another Wildcat layup attempt into the fourth row of the bleachers. "Don't come into my house. I'll send you away like a door-to-door salesman!" Big high-fived Trevor and gave a head butt to the bald Morrison in celebration.

It was not like Big to trash talk on the court, but every Bear was in high gear right now and the intensity was unbelievable.

With eight minutes left in the game, the Bears had

pulled even with Cartier Academy, knotting the score at forty-eight.

On the bench, Coach Kenny was in a frenzy, waving a rolled-up piece of paper and shouting at his players. It was all for show, however. No one was listening to him on the court, and Coach Kenny didn't dare make any substitutions. The five players he had on the court were getting the job done and he only hoped that they could bring home the win.

For the next few minutes, the two teams traded punches like a couple of heavyweight fighters in a slugfest. Neither one was prepared to back down. The Bears were passing the ball around like they never had before. Without a doubt, Langdon was still their go-to guy, but Chip, Trevor, Big, and Morrison were all making their shots.

Coming down the floor, Chip worked the ball around the perimeter. On the far side of the court, Trevor had managed to get a step on his defender and was crying for the ball. Chip zipped a pass to his friend who quickly nailed the open jumpshot. The Bears bench let out a shout of joy. The Grizzly Bears had taken the lead.

Cartier Academy was having some problems. They had expected to blow out the rag-tag little school from Cape Breton and hadn't quite prepared themselves mentally for the game. Now, with time winding down and the Bears with the lead, the Wildcats were starting to feel the pressure and beginning to bicker with each other.

Seeing that his team was in trouble, the Cartier Academy coach called a time out. As the Bears' starters approached the bench, the other players cleared a place for them to sit. No one bothered to take a seat. They were all too pumped.

"All right, guys," Coach Kenny hollered, rubbing the shiny heads of Trevor and Langdon. "If they make this free throw we're going to the one-three-one press." He glanced at Chip, who smiled.

"Definitely. Good call, Coach," Chip replied.

"We're only up by four," Coach Kenny continued. "Morrison, Big, let's set some picks and let Langdon get off some open shots."

Morrison and Big nodded their understanding.

"Langdon," Coach Kenny turned to the Bears' hot forward. "Hit your shots."

Langdon grinned.

Checking the clock, the Bears knew that if they could just hang on for another three and a half minutes, they would be provincial champions.

With the Grizzly Bears in possession of the ball, Chip positioned himself on the left side of the hoop and frantically waved for Langdon to pop up to the top of the key. Big, seeing Chip's direction, rushed up and set a pick for the Bears' shooter. Langdon cut to the top of the key, but the Wildcats had rotated on defence and now another Cartier Academy defender was glued to Langdon. Morrison, working the high post, quickly stuck his butt out and bumped the Wildcat, springing Langdon free as he curled around the top of the key to receive Chip's pass and drain the open jumper.

"Nice screen!" Langdon called, slapping five with Morrison and Big on the way down the court.

Inbounding the ball quickly, Cartier Academy pushed their offence down the floor and dropped the ball to the tall, burly player Morrison was guarding. The Wildcat wasted no time hooking his arm around Morrison's waist and leaving the Bears' player pinned to his hip as he spun to the hoop.

Big, seeing Morrison was beaten, rotated over to help out. Leaping across the key, Big slapped away the layup attempt, but as he landed, Big felt a horrible snap in his left foot.

"Ankle," grimaced the large boy as he rolled around on the floor.

The referee quickly stopped play and Coach Kenny rushed onto the floor to attend to his injured player. Big's face was contorted in pain. That was it for the Bears' big man. As the large centre hobbled to the bench with the help of his teammates, Coach Kenny winced visibly and called Taps off the bench.

"Taps," instructed Coach Kenny urgently. "Pass the ball as soon as you touch it. Don't shoot unless you are right under the basket and no one is around you. Got it?"

Taps nodded nervously. He had barely played in a

game all season, let alone being called off the bench for crunch time in the biggest game of the year!

Without Big clogging up the middle, the Wildcats scored three easy layups on the next few possessions. Then Chad drained a long-range three-pointer right in Chip's face to put the Bears down by three points with only a minute left.

The crowd, always loving an underdog, was going crazy cheering for the little team from Cape Breton.

Coming down on the attack, Chip slowed the offence and looked over his options. Seeing that Langdon had his defender stuck to him like Velcro, Chip swung the ball over to Trevor who immediately had his man in his face, denying him the jumpshot.

Trevor rotated the ball into the far corner where Taps was standing near the three-point line. Taps had actually moved out of position with the hope that no one would find him standing in the corner. No such luck. Seeing the pale, skinny boy with the ball, the Wildcat defender immediately backed off, daring Taps to shoot the ball.

"Taps, Taps, Taps!" shrieked Chip, begging for the ball back at the top of the key.

"Shoot it, shoot it, shoot it!" the crowd chanted.

Taps was in shock. He looked around blankly and vaguely saw his teammates waving for the ball, but it was clear that nothing was registering. Finally, in an act of desperation, Taps cocked the ball down by his hip and launched an awkward-looking three-pointer.

The shot had so much arc the ball almost got caught in the rafters. Hanging in the air for what seemed like an hour, no one could move. As the ball began its descent, time stood still. Everyone stared as finally the ball reached the orange iron rim.

Nothing but net.

The crowd went nuts. Morrison raced over and hugged Taps, who still had his arm extended. It was quite possible that the Bears' twelfth man still hadn't realized that he had scored.

"It's not over," yelled Chip, seeing that neither team had a time out left. The score was deadlocked at fifty-six apiece.

The clock had under thirty seconds left as the Wildcats came down for what could be the last possession of the game.

Seeing the clock winding down, Chad dribbled patiently at the top of the circle.

"Come on, cheesecake!" taunted Chip, slapping the gym floor with both hands and taking a low defensive stance. "Take it to me! Show me what you got!"

Chad wasn't buying, however, dribbling the ball with a slow, easy rhythm. The Wildcats would obviously wait until time had almost expired and then hope to score without leaving the Grizzly Bears enough time to get another attempt.

As Chad surveyed his options, his loose, easy dribble

got a little too easy. With cat-like quickness, the compact Chip extended his arms and tapped the ball away from the careless Cartier Academy guard.

Stumbling after the loose ball, Chip quickly regained his balance and was off to the races.

Cutting to the middle of the court, Chip saw Langdon burning down the floor on his right. To his left, Morrison was doing his best to keep up with the fast break. There were two Wildcat defenders in front of them and only about five seconds left on the clock.

A classic three-on-two fast break. Chip knew that the game would be decided on this one play. Not wanting to make his pass too early, he checked again for his teammates. Morrison was trailing badly and the second Wildcat defender had snuck over to cover Langdon.

Langdon was waving for the ball, but with the Cartier Academy player so close, Chip couldn't fire a clean pass to his wing man without the risk of it getting picked off. Chip had to find another way of getting the ball to his teammate.

As soon as Chip reached the top of the three-point line, he glanced at Langdon and pointed to the ceiling.

Langdon nodded as Chip stopped on a dime and lobbed a high ally-oop pass just to the right of the rim. If Langdon was going to get the ball he was going to have to go up in the air and get it!

Narrowing his eyes, Langdon took two long, powerful strides before launching himself skyward. Rising higher and higher, Langdon's altitude quickly left his earth-bound defender far below. The Bears' star extended himself and managed to catch the ball just as it passed inches over the rim. Cupping the rock between his fingers and wrist Langdon slammed home the ball with authority just as the final buzzer sounded.

Swinging on the rim for good measure, Langdon let out a long, loud shout of joy. The sound was drowned out by the cheering of the people in the stands and the rest of the Grizzly Bears as they swarmed onto the court.

The Grizzly Bears had won!

Jumping up and down, delirious with happiness, the teammates collected under the basket to celebrate. Even Big, sore ankle and all, hopped out to slap high-fives with the rest of the guys.

Langdon caught Chip's eye from across the mob.

"Nice pass!" he shouted reaching out to shake Chip's hand.

"Nice dunk!" Chip replied, shaking Langdon's before reaching up and rubbing the tall boy's shiny head.

"Hey, Big," Chip yelled at the limping Big. "By the way, did we ever get our biology project done?"

"Yeah," Big laughed. "'We' got it done."

Chip smiled. "See, I told you it wouldn't be a problem to get into the library."

Big grinned and play-punched his teammate as the stocky point guard was hoisted onto Trevor's shoulders.

"Hey, Coach," cried Chip, smiling and waving at

Coach Kenny who was slapping backs and shaking hands as if he was a politician.

"What do you want, Carson?" Coach Kenny said, trying to be gruff.

"This is fun, huh?"

"Yeah," Coach Kenny replied, breaking into a wide grin. "We really must do it again some time."

Chip grinned. "How about next year?"

Coach Kenny grinned back. "Definitely."

★ ★ ★

"Well, did you do it?" asked Trevor, propping himself up in the vinyl bus seat.

"Mission accomplished."

The Bears were bouncing along the highway en route to Cape Breton Island, anxious to get home and start savouring the hero's welcome they were sure to receive.

"When will he find it?" Trevor giggled.

"Oh, in about three . . . two . . . one . . . now!"

"Yuuuuuuuucckk!" shouted Chip Carson from his seat on the bus. "Whoever put Jello in my hat is going to get it!" The Bear point guard hopped out of his seat and started waving his Chicago Bulls cap in the air. The ball cap had a purple layer of slime on the inside and Chip had matching Jello trickling down his scalp. "Langdon, I'm going to get you for this!"

Langdon and Trevor had long since cracked up.

"Nicely done," laughed Trevor, slapping five with Langdon.

Chip smiled and licked some Jello off his hat. "Just 'cause you can dunk doesn't mean you can get away with everything."

"Hey, he's also the MVP of the tournament," piped up Big, who was taking up two seats in the back of the bus as he stretched out his injured foot.

"Yeah, I'm the MVP," Langdon said, waving a trophy in the air. "But I had to make a correction on the nameplate of the trophy."

"What do you mean?" Chip asked.

"Here." Langdon flipped the trophy to Chip.

Examining the front of the award, Chip saw what Langdon was talking about. Right under the words, *Most Valuable Player*, Langdon had pried off the metal plate with his name on it and scratched into the wood, *The Grizzly Bears.*

Chip looked at Langdon. "I think we should put this with the other piece of hardware," he said finally, pointing at the large championship trophy which was riding in the seat next to Coach Kenny. "Thanks, Langdon."

"Just for the record, we're the only team to win the provincial title with zero regular seasons wins," called Taps from the back of the bus. He was busy writing down all the statistical records the Grizzly Bears had broken on their two-day run to the provincial title.

"We're the only team to score less than six points in a half and come back to win the game. Big is the only centre to have eight blocks in one game."

"Big is the only centre to have eaten eight meals in that cafeteria," laughed Chip, "and survived."

"We had the most three-pointers in a championship game. No team has ever caused more turnovers in the last four minutes. We're the only team . . ."

As the bus drove into the night, Taps continued to rhyme off meaningless statistics and figures. The one fact that no one was about to forget, however, was that twelve individuals had come together as friends and teammates in those last two days, and had realized that sometimes what is on the stat sheet doesn't matter as much as what is in your heart.

"You know," Morrison mused to no one in particular. "I think I'm going to get a nose ring . . ."

MORE SPORTS, MORE ACTION
www.lorimer.ca

CHECK OUT THESE OTHER BASKETBALL STORIES FROM LORIMER'S SPORTS STORIES SERIES:

Camp All-Star
by Michael Coldwell

Jeff's been invited to an elite basketball camp, and he's looking forward to some serious on-court action for two weeks straight — but Chip, his completely unserious new roommate, seems to have other ideas...

Fast Break
by Michael Coldwell

Meeting people in a new town is hard. So when Jeff runs into a group of guys who love basketball as much as he does, he makes sure to stick with them when school starts. But at school, he finds out what they're really like...

Free Throw
by Jacqueline Guest

When his mother remarries, suddenly everything changes for Matt: new school, new father, five annoying new sisters, and even a smelly new dog. Worst of all, if he wants to play basketball again, he'll have to play with his old team's worst enemies.

Home Court Advantage
by Sandra Diersch

Life as a foster child can be tough — so Debbie has learned to be tough back, both at home and on the court. But when a nice couple decides to adopt her, Debbie suddenly isn't so sure of herself — and her new teammates aren't so sure about her either.

Fadeaway
by Steven Barwin

Renna's the captain of her basketball team, and is known to run a tight ship. But then a new girl from a rival team joins. Suddenly, Renna's being left out and picked on by her own teammates. Can she face this bullying and win her team back before it goes too far?

Out of Bounds
by Sylvia Gunnery

As if it isn't bad enough that Jay's family home has been destroyed by fire, Jay has to switch schools — which means he has to choose between playing for the enemy, and not playing basketball at all. And he can't decide which is worse.

Personal Best
by Sylvia Gunnery

Jay finally gets to go to Basketball Nova Scotia Summer Camp, and he even gets to stay in a real dorm with his best friend, Mike. But Mike's older brother is also there, and he's not exactly acting like a good coach or a good big brother... .

Queen of the Court
by Michele Martin Bossley

Kallana's father has suddenly decided that joining the basketball team will be a "character-building" experience for her. But she can't dribble, she can't sink a basket, and worst of all, she will have to wear one of those hideous uniforms…

Rebound
by Adrienne Mercer

C.J.'s just been made captain of the basketball team — but her teammate, Debi, seems determined to make C.J. miserable. Then C.J. wakes up one morning barely able to stand up. How can she show Debi up when she can't even make it onto the court?

Slam Dunk
by Steven Barwin & Gabriel David Tick

The Raptors are going co-ed — which means that for the first time ever there will be *girls* on the team. Mason's willing to see what these girls can do, but the other guys on the team aren't so sure about this…

Triple Threat
by Jacqueline Guest

When Matt's online friend, Free Throw, finally comes to Bragg Creek for a visit, the first thing they do is get a team together to compete in the summer basketball league. Unfortunately, Matt's arch-enemy has had the same idea…